To Eric,

N4mbers

N4m6ers

DAVID A. POULSEN

DUNDURN
TORONTO

Design: B.J. Weckerle
Cover design: Laura Boyle
Cover image: © kevinhillillustration/istockphoto.com
Printer: Webcom

Library and Archives Canada Cataloguing in Publication

Poulsen, David A., 1946–, author
Numbers / David A. Poulsen.

Originally published by Key Porter Books, 2008.
Issued in print and electronic formats.
ISBN 978-1-4597-3248-3 (pbk.).—ISBN 978-1-4597-3255-1 (pdf).--
ISBN 978-1-4597-3256-8 (epub)

I. Title.

PS8581.O848N85 2015   jC813'.54   C2015-901309-7
                                             C2015-901310-0

  2   3   4   5   19   18   17   16   15

  Canada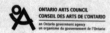

We acknowledge the support of the **Canada Council for the Arts** and the **Ontario Arts Council** for our publishing program. We also acknowledge the financial support of the **Government of Canada** through the **Canada Book Fund** and **Livres Canada Books**, and the **Government of Ontario** through the **Ontario Book Publishing Tax Credit** and the **Ontario Media Development Corporation**.

Care has been taken to trace the ownership of copyright material used in this book. The author and the publisher welcome any information enabling them to rectify any references or credits in subsequent editions.

— J. Kirk Howard, President

The publisher is not responsible for websites or their content unless they are owned by the publisher.

Printed and bound in Canada.

VISIT US AT

Dundurn.com | @dundurnpress | Facebook.com/dundurnpress | Pinterest.com/dundurnpress

Dundurn
3 Church Street, Suite 500
Toronto, Ontario, Canada
M5E 1M2

To my UBC classmates:
Jennifer Coloyeras, Sue Fast, and
Laura Trunkey — and the amazing mentor/leader/
friend — Glen Huser.
All of you made this so much more.

And to my family —
my mom, my wife Barb, Murray, Kim, Dillan, and
Chloe; Amy, Dan, Brennan, Kyle, and Gabriella;
Brad, Nicole, and Gracie —
your love lifts me higher.

Bidwell

MARCH 8, 1949

The Bidwell Gas Plant blew up at 5:43 p.m. on March 8, 1949, the result of what investigators discovered was a leaky gas valve. It was a Monday — a cold, not-winter-not-yet-spring prairie day with a bitter wind blowing hard out of the north. The wind made fighting the fire that followed the explosion a dangerous and nearly impossible task. Four people died that day: two fire fighters, one plant worker, and a fourth person whose identity was never known, the body burned beyond recognition and no identification found at the scene. Speculation was that this final fatality was a travelling hobo who had been sleeping inside the plant — the papers called it a classic case of being in the wrong place at the wrong time.

A fifth person, a twenty-four-year-old janitor's assistant, was rescued by a young secretary who had been working late in the office. She had managed to escape the inferno, but came back when she heard the man's

7

terrified screams. The assistant's leg had been badly shattered in the initial explosion and he would have perished had the young woman not gone back into the plant. Though small, the secretary managed to half-drag/half-carry the injured man away from the building. Once outside, the pair received help from passers-by who had stopped to watch the fire.

For weeks the story of the Bidwell Gas Plant explosion was front-page news across the country. People read the Bidwell accounts even before they turned to the stories on the situation in Korea; an international conflict that some were predicting would become a major war. The young secretary, who was hailed as a heroine for rescuing the injured man, became a household name. The Happy Gang, *Canada's most popular radio program, spent five entire minutes talking about the heroics of Julia Meyer.*

But eventually, as with all stories like it, the Bidwell explosion was replaced by other news, other stories. The Happy Gang *went back to jokes and songs, and Canada went to war in Korea. No one talked about the explosion anymore, and Julia Meyer passed into history.*

Today, no plaque marks the spot where the plant once stood and most people have either never heard of that March day more than sixty years ago or have long forgotten it.

Most people. But not all.

SEPTEMBER

One

One year ago, almost to the day ...

Forty-five seconds left.

Sweat, energy, and thinking: The three ingredients for a wrestler's success. Our coach, Mr. Findlay, must have said that maybe fifty times a practice. "Sweat, energy, and thinking, Crockett," he'd yell. "Give me those three things, I'll give you a win."

I looked at the other kid and I could see it in his eyes. I had him. We both knew it. Sweat, energy, and thinking. I wondered what my opponent's coach said to him. What if he said the same thing as Mr. Findlay? What if he said, "Give me those three things and I'll give you a win." One of those coaches would be lying.

Forty seconds. I was ahead on points. All I had to do was stay out of trouble and it was mine. *He* was mine. I moved in on him. I knew I didn't have to — I already had it in the bag — but the guy was done. I could see that. There was another point or two there for the taking, and I decided to take them.

Thinking, Crockett … thinking, Crockett … thinking, Crockett.

Then it happened. I still don't know how. I swear to this day the kid wasn't that good. I went in low for a single-leg takedown. I'd done it so many times. It had worked so many times. It had worked *in this match*. I'd taken him down with that move in the first minute and it was there again, I was sure of it. *I go in low, wrap that leg, bring it up, he goes down, and I've got him.*

It couldn't fail.

Could not fail.

But it did. The guy made a countermove. I'm not sure exactly what he did.

But he pinned me and that was that.

Sometimes I think it might have been different if I'd won that semifinal match at regionals. I might have been noticed by kids who weren't in The Six. Maybe even liked by a few. You can't be sure about something like that, but it always seems like the guys who are good at sports and who actually *win* are really popular.

But maybe I'm imagining the whole thing. I mean, maybe most of the school would have ignored me no matter what happened in that match. And maybe Mr. Retzlaff would've started the unit on the Holocaust the very next Monday even if I *had* won. And even if the kid who beat me hadn't been named Julius Epstein.

Which is a Jewish name. At least the Epstein part. I don't know about Julius. The only other Julius I've heard about got stabbed by a bunch of pissed off Romans in a Shakespeare play. I think there might be a few athletes named Julius, but I'm not even sure about that.

All I know is that Julius Epstein beat me. In the regionals. And my life changed after that day.

Two

The Six.

No mystery to the name. There were six of them.

There was Hennie, who broke a kid's nose for making a joke about his name; Jen, who made out with at least half the guys in tenth grade; Lou, the total klepto who stole money out of his mother's wallet even when he didn't want to buy anything; Big Nose Kate, whose nose wasn't big and whose name wasn't Kate — it was Sarah; T-Ho, who was the toughest of The Six and the leader and hated everybody who wasn't exactly like him; and Rebel, who wore the same black toque every day of his life and spoke about five words a month.

Some people said I was the seventh kid, and I guess I was. Of course, being the seventh member of a group called The Six isn't a real big deal. And every once in a while The Six, especially T-Ho, would make sure I knew I wasn't a *jen-yoo-wine* (that's how he said it) member of the group.

My name's Andy Crockett, but at our school not

many people get called by their real names. Since my last name's Crockett, my nickname is Alamo, which only makes sense if you know some Old West history. I guess Jen is up on her Old West history because when I moved to this school halfway through grade nine and people found out my name, she decided I was Alamo. (Davy Crockett, the Alamo — freaking brilliant, isn't it?) At least Alamo is a better name than Big Nose Kate, which was another one of Jen's creations. She came up with that after reading some Old West magazine. The real Kate was a prosititute and the girlfriend of Doc Holliday. I never did figure out the connection. When I asked Jen about it, all she said was, "Think about it, Alamo, think about it." So I thought about it ... and I still don't get it. I figure Jen's just weird. Horny and weird.

Seven of us. Or six plus one. We weren't really a gang, just people who liked being with each other better than with anybody else in the school. We weren't goths or even big-time druggies. Not really. Mostly we just couldn't stand the rest of them. We didn't fit in with the jocks (even though I was on the wrestling team), we weren't down with the skaters, and our grades made damn sure we didn't hang with the brains.

So it was sort of a process of elimination. And it had been that way since junior high, which is apparently when The Six sort of came together. Even though I came later, they let me hang out with them, mostly because I could get my dad's car once in a while, if T-Ho's Crap Wagon wasn't running. I had my learner's and T-Ho had his license but even so, Dad only let me take the car a few times. Actually I was never even sure that any of The Six liked me, or that I liked them. But when you're in a new school you want to hang out with somebody, and The Six were about the only people who talked to me at first.

Actually it was dog shit that did it. My first day in a new school and I somehow managed to step in a large fresh mound between where my dad dropped me off and the side door of Parkerville Comprehensive High School. Sweet.

Well, actually not so sweet. I scraped it off as best I could but there I was in my first class — math — and I smelled like — well, dog shit.

There was one kid, one of the brains — Kevin Rayburn — who was sitting in the next row. He made a big deal out of getting up out of his desk and moving to a desk on the other side of the classroom. The teacher looked at him and Rayburn (I found out his name later) said, "I can't see the board, there's a reflection or something."

Every kid in the class knew what was going on and a few of them laughed. That pissed me off.

So I gathered up my books, got up out of my desk, sauntered across the room, and sat right behind reflection boy. I stretched my feet out beside my desk and as far forward as I could. When the teacher looked at me, I said, "He's right, sir, that reflection is a killer over there. This is way better."

And that was it. When I walked out of the classroom, two guys and a girl were waiting for me. Turns out it was T-Ho, Rebel, and Jen. T-Ho punched me on the arm and said, "That was pretty good. Come on out to the parking lot after school. We're going to the DQ. You can catch a ride."

Then the three of them turned and headed off to their next class without waiting for me to answer. And that was it. I was the seventh kid in The Six.

You'd probably think The Six would all look alike, dress alike, have the same jewellery attached to the same parts of their bodies — that kind of stuff. You'd be wrong. Hennie's black and the best guy at a party — the man's hilarious. Lou's the tallest, over six feet, but he maybe weighs as much as me and I wrestle in the 145-pound weight class. He's got acne pretty bad, too. Jen would be gorgeous if she tried harder. She's tall, has a better than decent body, and great skin. If she smiled once in a while she'd get even more guys into the sack than she does without smiling. And she has blond hair, which is a weakness of mine. Except you know how some people have dirty blond hair? Well, Jen has blond hair that's dirty. That's what I mean about trying harder.

Big Nose Kate isn't gorgeous, even though *she* tries really hard. What I like about her is that she dresses like she's from another time period — or maybe another planet — and doesn't give a rat's ass what anybody thinks about it.

T-Ho's big and tough — a redneck and a farm boy all the way. And Rebel … he's hard to describe. Thing is, he looks too old for high school. He's about the same size as me but old-looking, and he always has his head partway down, like it's too heavy to hold up or

17

something. Which means that when he looks at you or talks to you he's sort of looking up through his eyebrows, if you know what I mean. But of course he doesn't talk to you very often, because he's Rebel.

That leaves me. Not as tall as I'd like to be, not as buff as I'd like to be, but what body I've got is in decent shape. I'm not pretty, but I'm not totally gross either … I don't think. I mean, girls don't fall over when I walk down the halls but they don't run and hide. (Except for dog shit day, of course.) Brown hair, blue eyes, high cheek bones, a wide mouth — too wide if you ask me. That's about it.

The thing is, I'm not my brother. If that sounds a little whiny and like I'm feeling sorry for myself, I guess I am. Tim is five years older than me. He's a better athlete, better looking — normal cheekbones and a normal-sized mouth and a smile that makes women go all stupid. He could give smiling lessons to Jen. Plus my brother's smarter and he knows more about cars. I'm catching up to him on that last one, but only because he's also a good teacher.

The rest of my family's just, like, you get used to them because they're your family, you know? My dad's an engineer with the power company, reads a ton of books, and is the eternal jokester. Once in a while he's pretty funny; the rest of the time we all get practice rolling our eyes. My mom works in a pharmacy (and rolls her eyes more than any of us at Dad's attempts at humour). If I was looking for a word to describe my mom it would be "nice," which every English teacher I've ever had has told me is a very boring descriptive

word. Apparently it doesn't "paint a word picture."
But screw it, she's nice.

And then there's Uncle Herm, the family embarrassment. He moved in with us just about the time I started grade ten. He got drunk the second day after he arrived and forgot to sober up. Dad told me that Herm, who is his younger brother by a couple of years, moves from one member of the family to another, stays for several months (or sometimes a year or two), then moves on. I guess it was our turn then. It could have been worse though. It's not like he was a mean drunk; he was just never sober. He'd have dinner with us most nights, then disappear either downtown to a bar or into the basement or out to our barn if the weather was okay. A bottle of rum later — off to sleep. It was the downtown nights that made him the family embarrassment because Dad would have to go get him. Uncle Herm was a big boy and Dad always needed help loading him into the pickup to get him home. It's funny how people with problems are pretty famous in small towns. Even people who had never met Uncle Herm knew who he was.

Actually, I lied about him being drunk all the time. There were a couple of times when we got into arguments about stuff; stuff I didn't think he knew anything about. I think he was more or less sober then.

We didn't do much — The Six — not at first. We hung out and listened to rap and hip-hop and, once in a while, a cool blues/rock group — somebody like the Black Keys — or maybe reggae, old Marley stuff or

Bedouin Soundclash. That was Hennie's influence. He's from Jamaica. Moved here when he was nine and even though he's been here seven or eight years he likes people to know he's Jamaican — and different. Still has the accent which, if you ask me, he exaggerates most of the time; got the dreadlocks, a different hat every day — none of 'em ballcaps. Hennie's not your typical small-town kid. But I guess none of The Six could be called *typical*.

We went to movies once in a while, too. The only one who smoked (cigarettes) was Lou. We all liked beer and Big Nose Kate was into tequila but it wasn't like we came to school drunk or stoned or got stupid every weekend. We just hung out. The others in The Six were together pretty well all the time. I had wrestling part of the year, so I wasn't with them quite as much.

One thing everyone at Parkerville Comprehensive pretty much agreed on when it came to The Six: We weren't what you'd call well-liked. Not The Six. And not me.

Three

About the third week of grade ten, we had to write an essay describing our school. The title of my essay was "Average."

That's because Parkerville Comp *is* average (notice I didn't say *nice*). It was average then and it's *still* average. We have okay basketball and football teams, an okay school band, and okay-looking girls. About what you'd expect for a small-town high school. We never win at the drama festival or the science fair, but we don't suck either.

Even the Parkerville building is, like, right down the middle. Low, flat, one storey, mostly brick, classrooms in two wings — one for niners and tens, the other for elevens and twelves. Walls painted beige. Art from the art kids on some of the walls. A big mural of a farm family stacking small, square hay bales takes up one whole wall down by the gym. That mural has been there for five or six years and the kid who painted it is like some major graphics guy in New York City. He's Parkerville's superstar grad. Which I don't figure counts for much. It's not like the guy is Sidney Crosby or Brad Pitt or something.

The school has its own smell. It's like when you're in a basement that's had water in it. Not a totally make-you-puke gross smell, just kind of old and musty, I guess. But it's no big deal. Forty-five seconds after you walk into the building in the morning, you pretty well forget about it.

Average school on an average street in an average town. Like I said, nothing exceptional about Parkerville Comprehensive. Except for Mr. Retzlaff.

Four

Except for Mr. Retzlaff.

It didn't take me long to figure out that Mr. Retzlaff was the coolest thing about Parkerville. Not cool as in flashy dresser, like some of the teachers, but not a sweat pants slob either.

First name Martin. All the kids called him Mr. R. It was his idea.

I'd say he was in his forties. Tall and fairly muscular, but not an athlete. He didn't coach any of the teams, but he came to more of our games than all the other teachers put together. Didn't matter what sport, you could look up in the bleachers or over at the sidelines and there was Mr. R.

He taught social studies and science. I didn't have him until grade ten, but I'd heard all about him from other kids. Everybody knew Mr. Retzlaff, and one of the things that made him cool was that he knew every kid in the school. You'd see him in the hall and even if you'd never met the guy he'd still say hi and call you by name. I never figured out how he did that. Parkerville isn't the biggest school around, but it isn't puny either. I bet there are five hundred students. Maybe Mr. R didn't know *every* name, but it sure seemed like he did.

So when I found out I'd have Mr. R for grade ten social, I was all, like, *yes!* I was kind of nervous, too. I really wanted Mr. R to like me. I think every kid in the school felt the same way. You were cool if Mr. R talked to you, smiled at you — liked you. And since everybody wanted to be cool, even The Six, it was a big deal to be liked by Mr. R.

Nobody — not even the kids who thought it was a blast if a teacher quit her job (like Miss Sawyer did last year) or took a couple of months off for stress leave (like the tall physics guy — I didn't know his name) — not even those kids messed around in Mr. R's class.

That first day was amazing. In only one class, Mr. R made me want to know everything there was to know about twentieth-century history from World War II on. We'd studied the first half of the century in grade nine and that had been baseball-bat-over-the-head dull. World War I, the Depression, William Lyon Mackenzie King — all of it a major snore.

Mr. R showed us this video he'd made of his most recent trip to Europe. It wasn't like some educational video. His commentary that went with it was hilarious. He had all these sarcastic comments about the people in all the countries he'd been to. Like they were the dumbest people on the planet. All of us were killing ourselves laughing.

But it wasn't *just* funny. It was like incredibly interesting. You actually *wanted* to watch it — and ask questions. I didn't ask any, though. I guess I was afraid of sounding as dumb as the people in the video.

Lots of kids did ask, though. Jen, who had been known to say fairly stupid things trying to be funny, was the first to put up her hand. "Mr. R, are the kids in those countries mostly like us or are they really different?"

Not a bad question.

Mr. R said something about kids being pretty much the same everywhere "except not as cool as Parkerville kids." We all laughed at that part.

There were lots more questions. I looked over at the other side of the room and T-Ho had his hand up. T-Ho — the kid who told me at the Dairy Queen the day of the dog-shit episode that the only bigger waste of time than school was "listening to the losers who asked questions *at* school."

But there he was — hand in the air. "I was wondering why people go to them other countries anyway. What's the point?"

Mr. R grinned. "Very good question, T-Ho. We go in part to see them — the country, the people, how they live … that sort of thing. And I hate to use this word, but it really is educational. There is a lot we can learn from seeing how other people did things in the past — that's what we call history — and how they do things now. Oh, and there are some terrific pubs and bars in these places too."

That had the class laughing again and even T-Ho was grinning back at Mr. R.

At the end of the class Mr. R stood at the door. As we were going out, he said, "Welcome to Social 10,

Mr. Mitchell" or "Miss Danforth" or whatever to each one of us. Again with the names. And I know for sure he got *those* names 100 percent correct.

When we got out in the hall, it was different than with most classes, where you're talking about food or what you're going to do after school or how stupid *that* teacher was. People were talking about France and Germany and Belgium. Yeah, I'm pretty sure that happens all the time in high school.

Jordie Carlton was the toughest kid in our school. Big and stupid tough. Nobody, including The Six — not even nose-breaking Hennie or T-Ho the Psycho — messed with this guy. Yet there was Jordie, talking about going to Europe someday to check out "that history stuff" like it was as important as his hopped up '85 Chevy pickup.

I could tell this was going to be the best school year ever.

And all because of social. Who would have thought *that* would be a reason to get up in the morning?

The thing is, you wanted to do great in Mr. R's class because you didn't want to disappoint him. And three weeks after I started in his class, I knew I'd disappointed him. I mean, it wasn't *in* class, but he was disappointed just the same. In me.

He was there at the wrestling regionals when I lost my match. The regionals were usually in the spring but there had been some problem that year so the tournament was put off until the following September. The start of my grade-ten year. Like I said, Mr. R was at most of our school's games and tournaments, so it wasn't any big surprise that he was at regionals or that he was the only teacher there besides Coach Findlay. After the match Mr. R came up to me. I figured he'd say the kind of stuff people say when you lose at sports — "You'll get 'em next time" or something like that. But that wasn't it.

"You shouldn't have let that guy beat you, Andy," is what he said.

"I know." I looked down at my feet like I suddenly needed to study my sneakers.

"No, you don't. You don't have any idea what I'm talking about, but one day you will. We'll talk about it and you'll understand." He started to walk away, but then he turned back. "The fall of the Alamo." He said it softly but I heard it. And the look on his face — not pissed off exactly but real serious — let me know he wasn't kidding around.

He turned and walked away again and this time he didn't stop or look back. So that's how I knew I'd disappointed him. I wasn't sure what he meant or what we'd be talking about "one day." All I knew is that I'd let Mr. R down and I felt pretty shitty about that. I decided right then I'd work harder than ever in his class, starting Monday.

Monday — that was the day we started the Holocaust unit. It wasn't actually called the "Holocaust Unit," it was just the war unit. But the Holocaust — that was the part everybody remembered.

Five

"Hey, Alamo."

I turned around. Hennie and Jen were leaning against the first floor lockers that ran along the wall next to Miss Van Tiegan's classroom. Physics. Miss Van Tiegan had replaced the tall guy who went on stress leave. Anyway, Jen was looking at me. Hennie had his earphones on and he was staring down at his iPod like it had rabies. I figured it wasn't working, but that didn't surprise me. Hennie was the kind of guy who would wear his watch into a swimming pool just to see what might happen then be pissed off when it didn't work after he got out of the water. Maybe he'd taken his iPod for a swim.

"Hey," I said back. I noticed Jen had done something different to her hair, but I wasn't sure what. It was just different. Streaks? Not great though. Maybe if she'd actually *finished* whatever it was she doing with the streaks. But, hey, at least it wasn't dirty. Or maybe the streaks were there to hide that part.

She must have noticed me looking at her 'do, because she shook her hair like a woman in a shampoo commercial as she spoke.

"Goin' to the dance?"

I shrugged. "Maybe. You?"

"Dude, we're all going."

Hennie straightened up and shuffled off down the hall, swearing at his iPod. Jen waited a few seconds then followed him.

That was it — the whole conversation. Most of the conversations between The Six were like that. A lot of raised eyebrows and body language — the biggest thing was to look bored. Jen had that part pretty well mastered. Except when she was hitting on a new guy, which tended to be on Fridays. Every Friday.

So I went to the dance. Before I tell you how it went, I guess I'd better mention Diana McNair, my ex-girlfriend who I was hoping wouldn't be my "ex" for that much longer. It was going to be a little tough to make happen, though. Of all the people in the school who didn't really like me, Diana *really* didn't really like me. I guess breaking up with girls some-times makes them feel that way.

It was stupid, I know that. *I* was stupid. I know that too. I think Diana liked me quite a bit and the thing is I liked her too — a lot. But it was the whole sex thing. I wanted it — she didn't. At least not as fast as I did. Which would have been okay if she hadn't already had sex with two other guys. She'd mentioned that one night when we were making out in the kitchen at her place. *In the kitchen.*

That's because her mom was in the living room so the couch wasn't exactly available. Plus it was a little tough to do the casual walk through the living room on our way to Diana's room, pretending we were just going up there to study. Yeah, Mom wasn't about to buy that. So we did our best with the counter in the kitchen. That's when Diana sort of announced that she'd been there and done that. A couple of times.

I was all like *cool, I'm fine with being number three as long as it's real freaking soon.* And that was the problem. Diana, the two-times non-virgin, wasn't on the same page when it came to just how far we would go.

A couple of weeks after the kitchen thing — one night while her mom was having a bath or something and we actually got to the couch — I was pretty sure it was about to happen. So I was a little surprised when Diana suddenly pulled my hand away from where it was totally enjoying itself and said, "Alamo, I'm not going to have sex with you. I like you and everything but I'm just not ready, you know?"

"No, I don't know," I said kind of loud. "What about before, with those other guys?"

"It was too fast both of those times. I wasn't ready then either but I let it happen and I wished after I hadn't. I don't want to feel like that again, okay?"

But like a jerk I kept trying, and talking, and trying some more. Not just that night but a lot of nights. Mostly I was just really pissed that I was still a virgin and she wasn't. I tried every ploy I could think of. I don't know if I really thought, "Do you realize I could be killed on my way home tonight and if that happens I'll die without ever having known the joy of yadda, yadda, yadda ... " could work, but that didn't stop me from trying.

It didn't work.

So I broke up with her. And I wasn't even cool about it. I said stuff I shouldn't have said and tried to make Diana feel totally crappy. Which I guess I did because she was crying when I left her house.

But afterwards, sad became mad and Diana did an excellent job of letting me know she hated me. Pretty much every day. And she made sure her friends hated me too. Which meant that there were even fewer people saying hi to me as I walked down the halls between classes. Counting The Six, the total number of people at Parkerville Comprehensive who actually talked to me was five. (I already explained about Rebel.)

And the worst part of it was that I wanted to get back with Diana. I knew I'd been a total creep and I felt bad about that. Plus I really liked her. Even without the home run. Besides, having a girlfriend was good. It made me feel, like, I don't know, like I fit in. Didn't matter though. Diana and I were done — forever.

School dances are like people. Some of them are boring. Some are anything but boring. And some try so hard not to be boring that they wind up being totally pathetic. The good thing is a dance can change. It just needs the right song at the right time, or the DJ to say something really funny or cool. That's all it takes to get everybody up off their chairs and moving.

That first dance of the year started out boring then moved directly to pathetic. First there were the decorations, which were totally stupid. They looked like they were for a Halloween dance, which this wasn't since it was only September. They were a cross between Dracula's castle and Madonna's bedroom — sort of sleaze with fangs.

There were those folding metal chairs all around the outside walls of the gym and some tables at one end — right under the fake fangs. The Six took over one of the tables, sat down, and waited for something — anything — to happen that might break the boredom.

As if the decorations weren't bad enough, the DJ was unbelievable. *This* DJ said a lot of things, but none of them were funny *or* cool. His name was Mighty Michael. The name alone ought to tell you right off that this was maybe the un-coolest guy ever to yell, "Parkerville, are you ready to *par-tay*?" into a microphone.

Then the dance changed. It suddenly became like the *Guinness Book of Records* all-time best dance ever, and a lot of it was because of Mr. R.

I was sitting with The Six and we were trying to decide whether to do a group hurl or hang Mighty Michael upside down from one of the basketball backboards. We figured we'd use the one sporting the cutout of a woman with bad hair wearing a black bra and a black cape — one of the classier decorations.

Anyway, that's when suddenly, like out of the

freaking blue, Mr. Retzlaff came over to our table and sat down in the only empty chair. He smiled and raised his glass of Coke, sort of like a toast to us and we all did it back.

"Pretty much sucks so far, doesn't it?" Mr. R waved his arm around the room.

We were all like, *yeah, totally.*

And that's when Mr. Tardif — the French teacher who you wouldn't think is cool at all — suddenly got up on stage and started doing a guitar-hero type performance to "Rock and Roll All Night." You know, the KISS song? And he was pretty good. I mean, all of us were a little embarrassed at first. Teachers are supposed to be … teacher-ish. Even Mr. R, who was so *not* like a teacher — even he didn't get up in front of the class and act like one of us.

But Mr. Tardif did. And after a couple of minutes, we were okay with it. And, like I said, he wasn't a bad Spaceman.

Mr. R watched and laughed like the rest of us. He made some pretty funny comments too, even though they were kind of hard to hear over the music. When the song was over and Mr. Tardif was bowing to the audience, Mr. R turned to us and grinned. "I used to have a dog with those same moves, but I de-wormed him and he's fine now."

We were still laughing when Mighty Michael grabbed the microphone and yelled, "I AM *DOWN* WITH THAT MAN" about fourteen times. Mr. Tardif walked off the stage and got high-fives from some of the other teachers and even a few students.

Mr. R didn't seem to be in any hurry to leave our table. By "our," I mean The Six table. The Six, for god's sake.

We didn't really know what to say to a teacher at a dance. I think we were still trying to deal with having a teacher — no, make that *Parkerville's coolest teacher* — sitting at our table. Finally Jen said something about how awesome social studies was. Not the best conversation starter, but at least she was making an effort.

But Mr. R shook his head. "No school talk. Tonight is about having fun. And I am DOWN WITH THAT."

We laughed pretty hard at that and Mr. R smiled and stood up. I thought he was leaving but he just turned the chair around and sat back down. Then he leaned forward on the back of it and looked at us. People all over the gym were checking us out; I knew that without even looking around. *Mr. R was hangin' with The Six, and people were noticing.*

The only thing was, if we weren't going to talk about school, we didn't really have much more to say. It got sort of awkward after a while. Finally, Mr. R said, "Okay, one last bit of school talk. You guys are really kickin' in social and I want you to know I appreciate it. Have a good time tonight." Then he stood up, turned the chair around again, and walked away.

I looked around the table. Every one of The Six were watching Mr. R walk across the gym. I mean *watching* him. And if we weren't already "kickin' in social," I can guarantee we would have been after his visit that night. What teacher *does* that?

Sure, some of them might brag up the preps and they might do it in the hallway at school or even in the lunch area. But Mr. R had come over to the seven people in the school who were least likely to win awards for brains or personality — *at the dance* — and pretty much told us we were cool.

Mighty Michael yelled, "I AM DOWN WITH THAT MAN!" one more time and this time I turned and grinned at him. (What the hell? He's a DJ ... he's *supposed* to be a dork.) I figured maybe the Retzlaff thing had been a sign. I mean, hey, if a guy like Mr. R was into The Six, then maybe I was on a roll. I looked over toward the stage at the other end of the gym where Diana McNair was leaning against the wall and drinking a lemonade with two girls who looked like niners. Diana was in grade ten, but God had decided she shouldn't be in any of my classes that year. What was that expression — the one about how absence makes the ladies miss the crap out of you? Something like that.

I walked over, took a Coke from the drinks table, and gave a buck to the nerdy kid in charge of refreshments, who looked like he thought his job was at least as important as, say, the guys who handle security for the Queen. Then I slow-strolled over to where Diana was missing the crap out of me. I stood there for a while before she even noticed I was there. I grinned at her. I hadn't really thought about what I'd say, so I just went ahead with the always brilliant, "Hey, Diana, what's happenin'?"

I knew from a couple of times in the backseat of T-Ho's Crap Wagon that Diana liked to talk dirty —

especially at *certain* times — but I wasn't quite ready for what came out of those Angelina Jolie lips right at that moment.

If Diana was missing me, she was amazing at dealing with her pain. Amazing and loud. What she said to me wouldn't have been so bad if her voice hadn't been a couple of decibels louder than Mighty Michael's. Diana still hated me, and everybody in the building — and maybe some people in buildings a few streets away — knew it. I wanted to at least walk away with some tiny shred of dignity so I waved and said "later" like everything was all cool. She told me where I could go and what I could do when I got there. Loudly.

I got the hell out of there and went back to The Six, where Big Nose Kate and T-Ho had seen (and heard) the little drama and were close to pissing themselves right there at the table. The rest of them were up dancing or in the can or something but it didn't matter. These two would be more than capable of making sure I didn't soon forget the Diana episode.

Big Nose Kate yelled, "She is *not* down with that man!" And when he was finally able to talk, T-Ho grabbed me by the shoulder so hard that it hurt and said "Another example of why you ain't *jen-yoo-wine*, know what I mean?"

Shit.

OCTOBER

One

I'd heard of the Holocaust before that Monday but it was just a word to me. I didn't know what it meant, not really. To be honest, I didn't know too many Jews. In fact, if you don't count *Seinfeld* re-runs and a few other people on TV, then Julius Epstein, the kid who beat me at the regionals, was the only Jew I'd ever met. I guess growing up in a small town like Parkerville isn't the best way to run into a lot of Jewish people. Or people of different colours and races generally. It wasn't like when we'd go into the city. There we'd see what my dad called diversity. Not a lot of diversity in Parkerville. I'm not sure why that is.

Like I said before, the unit wasn't called the "Holocaust Unit." That was our name for it. But not even right away. Most of the kids knew as much about the Holocaust as I did — not much. So that first day, it was like totally new information for a lot of us.

The class started with Mr. R pointing stuff out on this wall map of Europe he had at the front. The map was faded and looked like it was at least as old as

Parkerville Comprehensive. It had marks pretty well everywhere and scribbled notes in just about all the ocean parts. There wasn't much blue on that map. Mr. R talked about how the borders of some of the countries weren't the same then as they are now. To tell the truth, it wasn't the most exciting few minutes. For a Mr. R class, it was getting awfully close to boring. But that didn't last long.

There was a quote in the top right hand corner of the blackboard in big block letters: "The Treaty of Versailles is a flagrant trampling of German rights and must be despised and resisted by every patriotic German." — Adolf Hitler

The quote hadn't been there last class so I figured it must have something to do with what we'd be talking about today. All I knew about Hitler was that he was like the most horrible leader there had ever been. I wondered about having a quote on the board from this guy who was supposed to be so terrible, but I figured Mr. R would explain. I looked around the room. Everybody looked like they were thinking the same thing I was: *So where is this going?*

Mr. R was always putting quotes on the board from people who were supposed to be totally disgusting, but sometimes what they said sort of made sense. And sometimes, he'd put quotes on the board from the people you thought were the good guys. Turns out they said some pretty creepy stuff. "It's never a good idea to make assumptions based on what people say or think." Mr. R said that a lot. I figured the quotes on the board were supposed to be examples of why you shouldn't make assumptions. At least that's what I thought. One of the things I liked about Mr. R was that he didn't always explain everything completely — he liked for us to figure stuff out for ourselves.

I'd guessed right. Mr. R left the map and walked over to where the quote was written on the board. He stood beside it looking at us.

"Adolph Hitler ... well, well, well. Mr. R must be losing it, right? He's got a quote from history's biggest monster on our chalkboard. What is going on?"

I looked around the room again. Some of the kids were smiling. I was too. Because that is almost exactly what I'd been thinking.

"Hitler, a monster? Maybe. But let's look at what he is saying here." And for the next few minutes Mr. R told us how the Treaty of Versailles — which was the peace treaty signed at the end of World War I — was unfair because it made Germany take the blame for the war and pay billions of dollars and have practically no army and lose a lot of its land and territories. You could see how the German people would be pissed off.

That whole class was about the treaty. Mr. R had photos of the Hall of Mirrors in the palace where it was signed and it was pretty interesting, I have to admit. And there were other images too. Some showed what Europe looked like after the World War I, a lot of rubble and destroyed buildings, even some dead bodies — I wasn't sure where he got those pictures, but they definitely got our attention.

But then the class got even more excellent. Mr. R got T-Ho and Marcia Kiefer, who was this pretty big but really popular girl, up at the front of the class. That blew me away. T-Ho? Not exactly the guy you'd figure Mr. R would pick to be the star of some class activity. The weird part was that T-Ho seemed more or less okay with it.

"Now, we're going to have a class exercise, a game if you like," Mr. R said. "I want all of you to pretend — remember I said *pretend* — that T-Ho (Mr. R was the only teacher who didn't call T-Ho by his real first name, which was Travis, middle name Howard — that's the *T-Ho* thing) and Marcia have had a terrible fight. Not a boyfriend-girlfriend type fight, just a huge and really ugly argument, and now they completely hate each other."

By then most of the class was laughing and Marcia's face was the colour of a stop sign. T-Ho didn't exactly look like he was having a great time, but he was definitely handling being up there in front of the class better than I thought he would. I mean, T-Ho's whole life is about being cool — and having a look on his face that says adults are stupid and since school was invented by adults — it's *really* stupid. But there he was at the front of Mr. R's class — and not hating it.

Mr. R held up his hands to get us to settle down. "Now the war between these two has been going on for a really long time and both of them have done some really nasty stuff to each other."

Then Mr. R got four other kids up at the front. One of them was Jordie Carlton, two were girls, and the other one was me. Mr. R lined the four of us up beside Marcia, which left T-Ho on the other side of the room, all by himself.

"Because of the intervention of these four people, who are Marcia's friends — in war they are called allies — T-Ho has lost his big battle with Marcia."

"Yeah, right," T-Ho sort of snorted like he was saying *yeah, that's going to happen*. Except he didn't push it too far, maybe because Jordie was one of the allies.

Mr. R walked over to the board. "What's going to happen next is that Marcia and the allies are going to decide all the ways they will punish T-Ho for having this big, long fight with Marcia. And we're going to write down all of these punishments in something we call 'The Treaty of Her Guys.'"

The four of us suggested stuff and Mr. R wrote our ideas on the board. We took away the Crap Wagon and made T-Ho give a couple of hundred dollars to Marcia, plus five bucks out of every nine dollars (an hour) he made pumping gas at the Jiffy Gas Mart on the highway for the next year. We decided he'd have to have one hand tied behind his back every day at school (that one was my suggestion). And the best one? Every time T-Ho saw Marcia in the hallway he'd have to say he was really sorry for all the pain he had caused her. Actually, I thought we did a pretty good job of coming up with stuff that was kind of like the things the Treaty of Versailles did to Germany. Mr. R must have thought so too because he was nodding and saying "good one" after most of our suggestions.

By the end of the exercise, I think T-Ho was starting to forget it was supposed to be a game. But actually it was cool. Mr. R asked Marcia and the four of us to sit down and kept T-Ho up at the front of the room.

"How do the rest of you feel about what has happened here?" Mr. R looked around the room. "Was it fair, for example, to take T-Ho's car?"

For a while, people tried to be funny. "If you really want to punish T-Ho, you should make him drive the Crap Wagon for the rest of his life." That was Hennie. There was more stuff like that, and then a couple of guys made suggestions about what T-Ho could do for Marcia that made Marcia's face get even redder. Mr. R didn't put up with that. "Mr. Brunt and Mr. Bonham, you'll wait in the hall until the class is over and then you will meet with me."

After they were gone, people got serious. "It wasn't fair what the five of them got to do to T-Ho." This came from a girl I didn't know who sat near the back of the class. Turns out that was about how everybody felt. Even Marcia — the "enemy" — said, "I think it was wrong to take his car. It would make it way too hard for him to get to work and school."

Mr. Retzlaff nodded. "Good point, Marcia. Never take a man's Crap Wagon."

That got a good laugh.

"But here's what's most important." Mr. R walked to the first row of desks. He looked at all of us and then back at T-Ho, who was still standing at the front of the class, his hands shoved into his jeans pockets.

"T-Ho, how do *you* feel about what happened here today?"

T-Ho didn't even hesitate. "I'd be taking as much time as I needed to get even with every one of those bastards."

A few people laughed, but not many. Mr. R smiled. "While I would have preferred it if he'd stated it a little less colourfully, T-Ho has expressed exactly what I think each one of us would feel in that situation. And for that, ladies and gentlemen, I believe T-Ho deserves a round of applause."

All of us clapped like crazy and T-Ho even got a high-five from Jordie on his way back to his desk. Mr. R walked back up to the board and pointed to the Hitler quote. "Think about it, people."

And then the bell rang — almost as if Mr. R had been able to make it happen right at that second. It was the perfect ending to a very amazing class.

Two

I had to face reality — Diana McNair was out of my life. I tried calling her a couple of days after the dance. She didn't hang up on me, but her voice told me that I was having about the same effect on her as, say, a bad smell.

I was pretty upset … for about a week. My brother, Tim, came over for dinner one night and told me I'd get over it. He was home for a few days from university. He was staying at his girlfriend's house so this was the first time I'd seen him. I don't usually listen to him about women issues since he's too old to have a clue how fifteen- and sixteen-year-old girls think (he's twenty-one), but this time he was right. Of course, he was just lucky, since he had no way of knowing about the beach volleyball game. Or Patti Bailer. That's because they hadn't happened yet.

The thing is I'm decent at beach volleyball. It's not like my *best* thing, but I can get through a game without embarrassing myself. Especially when the other players are The Six and their athletic abilities add up to a number that rhymes with schmeero.

It was Jen's idea. "It's our last chance to catch some rays, drink a few beers, and have some fun."

She was right. It was like a seriously hot fall day and Dad let me have his car so we had that *and* the Crap Wagon. We swam in Scout Lake, which isn't very big. My dad, who's taken me fishing there for years, says that's why the water is so warm. It's an awesome looking place — the kind you see in those service station postcard pictures. The lake is surrounded by huge spruce and pine trees that must be a hundred years old.

There's tons of sand at one end of the lake and that's where we set up for the afternoon — blankets, beer, chips, dip, a portable volleyball net that Hennie bought at a garage sale a couple of months earlier. One of the weird things about Hennie is that the guy goes to garage sales just about every Saturday, sometimes in Parkerville, sometimes in the city. And he buys all this stuff that I'm pretty sure he'll never use. T-Ho gives him a hard time — calls Hennie a "garage sale Grandma" — but it doesn't bother Hennie. He keeps going to sales and buying. And one of the things he bought was the volleyball net.

It was excellent. We played two games and I was a stud in both. Even Rebel said "impressive" after I smashed one down Big Nose Kate's throat. T-Ho and Rebel and the two girls were on one team. Hennie, Lou, and me — we were the other team. We killed them.

We were in the middle of high-fiving and punching air and stuff after the second game when I saw this

47

girl — one I'd never seen before. She was sitting up by the trees that bordered the beach. I wasn't sure how long she'd been there. I guess with the game going on I didn't see her at first. She was putting on sun block and pretty much ignoring us, which couldn't have been easy since we were fairly loud.

I couldn't tell for sure if she was *totally* hot, since she was a ways away, but she definitely looked promising. I kicked the ball over to where she was sitting and then raced to get it before anybody else could.

Smooth.

It would have been smoother without all the stuff everybody was yelling, which pretty much ruined any chance I had of making the whole thing look accidental. It's hard to be cool with a girl when lines like "Don't tell her about your genital warts" and "Virginity is not the answer" are ringing through the trees. There was more, but you get the idea.

I thought about grabbing the ball and going back to The Six without saying anything to her but I figured that would look even dumber. When I got closer, I could see I'd been right about the hot thing. But she didn't look "duh" gorgeous, you know? Like those girls who spend a few hours every morning working on their faces and hair and haven't ever read a book or had a thought that doesn't start with "How do I look?" They always have that *where am I and what day is this?* expression on their faces.

This girl seemed … I don't know … together.

"Hi," I said. Amazing opening line.

She looked up from putting lotion on her legs. "Hi."

I picked up the ball and stood there for a while trying to ignore all the stuff that was still coming from the beach. "Loser" seemed to be the current favourite.

Which wasn't helping my confidence. Plus I was wishing I'd spent more time deciding what I was going to wear that day. I had on this stupid T-shirt Uncle Herm had given me for my last birthday. It had "Beer — It's What's for Dinner" written across the front. Uncle Herm thought it was hilarious. Yeah, thanks, Unc … I'm pretty sure this shirt is totally impressing this girl. Right up there with the genital warts.

"You … uh … go to Parkerville?"

"I will be. I start next week."

"Oh."

The "loser" thing was a chant now and quite a bit louder. Sweet.

"We just moved here," she said.

"Oh … uh … yeah, well, I'll probably see you around school then."

"Probably."

"I'm Andy Crockett. People call me Alamo." I set the ball down and started to put my hand out but then I thought about how The Six would deal with that and changed my mind.

"I'm Patti Bailer. People call me Patti."

At first I thought it was a put down, or that she was being sarcastic, but she was smiling, so maybe not.

"Cool. Well, I'll see you at school then." As soon as the words were out of my mouth, I remembered I'd just said the same thing five seconds earlier.

"Great."

"Great."

And it *would* have been great if I'd remembered to take the ball with me when I went back down to the beach.

Shit.

On the way back to town, T-Ho stopped the Crap Wagon right next to this field. I pulled up behind him, trying to figure out what was wrong. T-Ho's car was actually running, so it didn't seem like there was any reason to stop. The only things in the field were some round bales of hay left over from the summer. Nothing else.

T-Ho and the others got out of his car and he motioned for Rebel and me to do the same. Major grumbling from The Six. Except for Rebel. To grumble you'd actually have to say something.

"Dude, did you like bump your head?" Jen stared at T-Ho. Of course nobody got *too* smartassed with T-Ho. Except for Hennie.

"Once a farm boy, always a farm boy, eh, brother? Just can't get enough of the smell of cow shit," Hennie gave a big sniff.

"If you shut up you might learn something." T-Ho looked at all of us but he didn't seem mad. Actually, he had a little smile on his face, like he was in on something and we weren't.

So all of us followed him down into this ditch, up the other side, and through a barbed wire fence. Rebel was right behind T-Ho, looking sort of … interested, which wasn't how Rebel normally looked.

I stepped on the middle wire and held up the top one like I'd seen people do in movies. Jen and Big Nose Kate got through without tearing any of their clothes and Big Nose Kate smiled at me. Then we all trooped along behind T-Ho out into the hay field for freaking ever.

I like the smell of pastures and hay fields and I liked this one a lot. Sometimes it feels good to get away from the smells of a town, even a small town — gasoline, garbage, fast-food joints. There weren't any of those smells here. Hennie jumped up on one of the round bales and took a couple of selfies up there. Lou pulled a stem of alfalfa out of the ground and stuck it in his mouth. It had dirt on it but Lou either didn't notice or didn't care.

There was a line of trees along one side of the field and the sun had dipped low enough in the sky that the light coming through those trees was making very cool geometric patterns on the ground all around us.

We kept walking and I kicked through the stubble down to the dirt in one spot and reached down and grabbed a handful. It reminded me of the smell when my dad and I dig our potatoes out of the garden. I was wishing the highway noise was gone and I even wished The Six weren't here. I'd have liked to hear silence in this place.

"Shit." Lou lifted a runner and examined the bottom of the shoe. So much for silence.

"Cow shit, to be exact," Jen laughed. "Who do you think you are … Alamo?"

Yeah, hilarious, Jen.

51

There weren't cows in the field now, but apparently there had been. T-Ho didn't pay any attention to the rest of us. He just kept walking like he was on some kind of mission. When he finally stopped, no one was sure why. There were chunks of cement foundation sticking out of the ground all over the place, like there'd been a building there once.

Rebel, who is curious about exactly nothing, asked, "So, what was it?"

"Bidwell Plant — gas or something. It blew up about sixty years ago. Some people died. Right here."

I looked at T-Ho but his face didn't tell me much. Like, was this a joke or serious or what?

"Did you know one of the people who died?" Hennie kicked at a chunk of cement and looked at T-Ho like, *Dude, are you okay?*

T-Ho started to shake his head then he stopped. "No ... no I don't ... I didn't ... I ... Christ, didn't I say it was sixty years ago?"

It wasn't what you'd call a real definite answer.

Jen had her hands on her hips. "And we should know about this, why?"

T-Ho shrugged. "Just thought you might like to have a little history about, y'know, where you live."

"So what are you, Mr. R?" Big Nose Kate was grinning. "Should we call you, like, Mr. T?"

"Shit, you guys. What losers!"

I couldn't tell from the way he said it if T-Ho was pissed off or what. I also wasn't sure what he wanted us to do with our little history lesson. I looked at the foundations some more and then back at him.

He shrugged a slow-motion shrug and started walking away. So what was the deal? Ghost story? They're way more effective at night. That couldn't have been it. So what then? It didn't make a whole lot of sense. My big question was how did T-Ho know all this stuff? T-Ho isn't a guy who spends a lot of time reading the newspaper or skimming through history books. And if this place was such a big deal to him, why hadn't it ever come up before? Like I said, it didn't make any sense. But I kept my mouth shut. T-Ho put up with some people giving him a hard time, but I wasn't one of those people. Besides, he was already half way back to the car. Rebel hung back kicking the cement foundations and looking around like he was one of the Hardy Boys, or a dude from *CSI*.

It was a day of surprises.

The following Tuesday Patti Bailer showed up in two of my classes — social and English.

There *is* a god.

Three

A four-door, six-cylinder, '58 Chevy Biscayne with 83,000 miles (it was an old speedometer — before kilometers). And next to making out with Diana McNair (and thinking about making out with Patti Bailer), that car was the best thing about being me.

I guess you could boil my grade-ten year down to four major deals: The Six, Mr. Retzlaff's social class, Patti Bailer, and the Biscayne. Not exactly huge stuff, but that's the way it is in grade ten. It's not like you're going to save the world or score a Stanley Cup–winning goal or drive a Testarossa. It's your friends, school, girls, and a car.

It was my brother Tim who taught me the whole business of restoring a car. The first one we worked on was a '59 Edsel. That was his, when he was still at home; he got it in grade ten — the year *he* had Mr. R for social. I probably wasn't much help since I was only about eleven at the time. But I remember both of us loving that car.

People sometimes wonder if Tim and I are really brothers. He's always been taller than I'll ever be. And he has those killer looks I mentioned before. Me, on the other hand? I have the kind of face that's perfect for reading the morning announcements. Also, Tim has darker hair; mine's more light brown. More ordinary.

My brother totally kicked butt all through school — still does, except now it's at university. I've never been a big school guy, at least not when it came to grades and stuff like that. Reading? Well, that's another thing entirely. You'd have to kill me to keep me from reading. I think I got that from my dad when I was little. My dad and I read together all the time. Sometimes he read my books and once in a while he'd let me read one of his murder mysteries. I remember how Dad would lie on the couch to read his book and I'd lie on top of him to read mine.

Sports — I already mentioned that, especially wrestling. But the rest of school, like say, math, chemistry, physics … pretty nasty.

So, yeah, I guess there are quite a few differences between Tim and me. But when we've got our heads under the hood of a car — especially an old car — we're definitely brothers. We'd spend hours fixing them up, then rodding around town checking out girls (well, Tim wasn't all that interested in that part since he's had this very hot girlfriend, Carmen, since about grade eight).

After the Edsel, we worked on a 1950 Ford pickup — sweet truck. Then came the Biscayne, which was *my* baby in grade ten. Tim helped me buy it at a farm auction sale for four hundred bucks. Not bad since it actually ran. I mean, it didn't run great, but you could maybe get around the block in it. I loved that car.

Every once in a while, someone would drop into Mr. R's class. Usually it was a former student, maybe passing through town on their way to some cool job. Mr. R always remembered the person's name. There was one guy who hadn't been in the school for six years and he knocked on the door, came in and there was Mr. R practically yelling, "Carl McOdrum! Come on in, it's been a long time." And ol' Carl, he came in and shook Mr. R's hand, then went to a desk at the back and sat there grinning, pretty much for the whole class. And the art guy from New York City — he stopped in one day too. Got two calls on his cellphone while he was there, which I figured would bug Mr. R but he seemed okay with it.

A few times people dropped in who were too old to be Mr. R's former students but were good friends of his. Even some famous guys. Like there was this one guy who looked familiar and it turned out he was a hockey broadcaster on TV. Then there was a big-shot politician — he came by a couple of times. He stood up front shaking hands with Mr. R and telling the class how we were the "luckiest kids in the whole district to have the opportunity to be in THIS MAN'S CLASSROOM." His voice went up at the end and I wondered if he'd ever heard Mighty Michael. I could hear kids whispering, "Hey, isn't that what's his name? Isn't he like some government guy or something?" I didn't have a clue who the guy was. I only watch the news when there's like a 9/11 event or when one of the musicians I like gets busted. Of course, I would have figured out who the guy was eventually because Mr. R had him up there at the front of the class for quite a while and was treating him like he was a president or a prime minister or something and I was pretty sure he wasn't either of those. I have to admit it was pretty awesome having all these people coming around. It made me realize Mr. R wasn't just cool. He was important, you know?

I was standing in the hall by my locker one day after class when Patti Bailer stopped as she was walking by. The student union president from a couple of years before had dropped in to social and even answered one of Mr. R's questions — something about Mussolini or somebody like that.

"You think he puts them up to it?" Patti asked.

"What? Puts who up to what?"

"You think Retzlaff gets those people to stop by and makes it look like it's just out of the blue?"

"Why would he do that?"

She shook her head. "I don't know. To impress us? Or maybe to show us how much he matters to them and *should* matter to us. You know, to get us to work harder and maybe be as successful as they are and some day a few years from now drop in on Mr. R's social class."

"You're kidding, right?"

"I don't know." Patti started off down the hall. "I don't know if I'm kidding or not."

Four

It was part way through the class. Social. We'd been working on a written response to some question — I think it was how we felt about the Americans not entering the war until it had been going on for a couple of years. Most of us had finished.

Kids were talking and shifting stuff around; there was some laughing, a few books crashing down on desks, the desks themselves scraping on the floor ... I was finishing off the last of a juice box, a couple of slurps at the end so I didn't miss any.

Usually Mr. R put his hands up or he'd say something and that would be our cue to cool it. But this time there was no signal. He just stood at the front of the classroom, looking at us. Not pissed-off looking at us — just looking and waiting. And it wasn't long before all the noise stopped and every eye in the room was on Mr. R. I wasn't sure how he'd managed to communicate that he wanted silence but he had — without saying, or really doing, anything. It was impressive.

"How many of you have heard of the Holocaust?"

A few hands went up. Some kids nodded, but didn't put up their hands. I figured maybe they were like me. I'd heard of it … I'd seen a movie or something a while back about some guy saving a bunch of his Jewish workers from the Nazis. The movie was okay, but I wasn't sure I'd be able to really explain what the Holocaust was.

"Louise."

"That's when the Germans — the Nazis — killed the Jews, like millions of them, right?"

Okay, I could have said that much. So maybe I *did* know what the Holocaust was, after all.

"Anyone else? Ben?"

Ben's a computer geek and a smart kid. I figured he'd have something to say.

"The Nazis had gas chambers. People were herded into them supposedly for showers and then the gas was turned on. Lots of others were shot and a bunch more went to concentration camps where they starved to death and stuff. It was something like six million Jews who were supposed to have died."

Mr. Retzlaff nodded. "Good." He looked at Ben and at Louise. "Excellent. Ben, you said 'supposed to have died.' Interesting choice of words. Your answers tell me you've read and listened to history."

"And seen the pictures," Patti said.

I looked over at her. She was leaning forward in her desk and looking at Mr. R. She looked … intense. It was the first time she'd said anything in social.

"And you've seen the pictures," Mr. R repeated. "Perfect."

59

He began walking up and down and rubbing his hands together. The great thing about Mr. R was that this stuff really got him excited. Plus, he could get us just as excited.

"That's what I want to talk about today. The pictures, the stories, the things you've read and heard about something that took place in the past … we call that history. Now some of you may have heard that the history of war is told by the winners. Can anyone see a problem with that?"

No response to that for a while. "Maybe you get a particular slant on what happened." Ben again.

"Ah ha," Mr. R nodded like crazy. "Let me ask you this. You've just fought a war with another country. You won, but a lot of your people died fighting in this war. If the historians are from the victors' side — your side, in this case — do you think they're going to spend a lot of time talking about what good guys the enemy were?"

Most of us shook our heads.

"Would you want them to?"

More head shaking.

"In fact, what you'd probably want is for the historians to paint as black a picture of the enemy as they can. I mean, if they weren't bad guys doing bad things, why did we fight with them, shoot them, blow them up … right?"

This time *we* were nodding. I'd been watching Patti Bailer. She hadn't been shaking her head or nodding. But she was shaking her head now. She raised her hand.

"Yes, Patti?"

"Why wouldn't the historians on the losers' side write their own account of the war?"

"Good question. They probably would. But do you think the conquerors are going to allow those accounts to ever see the light of day ... accounts that point out what bad guys *the winners* were and what good folks the defeated enemy actually were? Not very likely."

Mr. R didn't say anything for a couple of minutes. He was letting us think about it.

He walked to the back of the class and then partway back to the front. He stopped. "So that takes us back to the Holocaust. The slaughter of six million Jews — I think that was the number you cited, Ben."

Ben nodded.

"And Patti referred to pictures."

Patti didn't say anything; she just stared at Mr. R.

Mr. R finished his stroll to the front of the classroom.

"And that's what we're going to talk about later this week," Mr. R was smiling. It was that I-know-something-you-don't-know smile, the smile that I had already figured out usually made for a very interesting class. "Pictures, war pictures, disturbing pictures — pictures that have upset people for several decades ... because everyone knows pictures don't lie. Right, Patti?"

Before Patti could answer, the bell rang and Mr. R headed for the door to say his goodbyes as we filed out of the classroom. As I headed out into the hall, I noticed his smile was even bigger than usual.

I was supposed to meet Lou after school that day. Probably wanted to borrow money. About the only time Lou talked to me was to ask for money. I don't know why, but Lou was the one guy in The Six I didn't really trust. Hennie and T-Ho were kind of scary sometimes and Jen was weird. But with Lou, it was like you didn't want to leave your wallet lying around. Maybe it was because he bragged about ripping off money from his mom's tip jar (she worked at a restaurant in town). I don't know, but I just didn't feel real comfortable around the guy.

Turns out I didn't have to worry about it since he didn't show. And when I asked him about it later he looked at me like I'd made the whole thing up. Which didn't help with the trust issue. It was actually kind of annoying, especially since I waited around for him for quite a while. I hung around behind the school throwing a football back and forth with a kid named Darryl who I'd seen in the halls. It wasn't often that people wanted to do anything with me, so tossing a football back and forth was like a major moment on my social calendar.

It didn't last long though. After a few passes, Darryl caught the ball, said "see ya tomorrow" and walked off. Yeah, a *major* social moment.

I reached down to pick up my backpack from the grass and when I looked up I saw something I didn't think I'd ever see: T-Ho and Rebel coming out of the school with Mr. R, one on either side of him. They were laughing like Mr. R was the funniest thing since Adam Sandler.

T-Ho wasn't exactly what you'd call a laugher. Except when *he* was the one saying stuff that was supposed to be funny. And I wasn't totally sure I'd ever seen Rebel smile. Something else I'd never seen was T-Ho and Rebel hanging around school after the last bell. Usually they were out of the building and into the Crap Wagon in about … fifteen seconds. Yet there they both were — still at school, walking with a teacher and acting like they were in the front row at some comedy club. Another amazing chapter in the book called *Mr. Retzlaff.*

All three of them disappeared around the corner of the building, heading for the parking lot. I thought about following them, but decided against it. I mean, it's not like they were doing anything wrong. Besides, if T-Ho saw me sneaking around spying on him and Rebel, the best I could hope for was a speedy recovery.

But I thought a lot about seeing the three of them like that. It was weird.

Still, when you added up everything about the day, I'd have given it a passing grade. Especially Mr. R's class. That night at the dinner table I told Mom and Dad and Uncle Herm about it. And about how I couldn't wait for the follow-up class when he talked about the pictures from the war.

"How cool is that going to be?"

Nobody answered. Dad looked at me and I thought he was going to say something, but he didn't. Mom seemed to be concentrating extra hard on her mashed potatoes. And Uncle Herm — nobody ever knew what he was thinking about.

Except I found out exactly what he was thinking later that night. I was outside changing the oil in the

Biscayne. It had only been maybe two weeks since the last time I changed it, but it gave me something to do with my car. Besides, I figured it was good practise for when the car actually *needed* to have the oil changed.

Uncle Herm wandered over as I was wiping oil off my hands. After he asked me a couple of things about the Biscayne, out of the blue he says, "I'd keep my head up around that Retzlaff bird if I was you."

Retzlaff bird. Uncle Herm talked kind of weird sometimes, so the "bird" thing didn't mean much. But what about the "I'd keep my head up" part?

I had no idea what I was supposed to say to that so I just looked at him.

"He's been peddling that garbage for years. The school board checked him out a while back. Didn't get him though, mostly because none of the kids would say anything. There's a few of those guys around — Holocaust deniers, they call them — and they're all full of shit but they've got lots of crap to back up their arguments. Just keep your head up, is all I'm saying."

I'd never heard the term "Holocaust denier" before. Hell, I'd just learned what the Holocaust actually was. Besides, Mr. R hadn't denied anything. He just questioned stuff and wanted us to do the same thing.

"Mr. R is an awesome teacher." I threw the oily rag down on the ground. "The best one I've ever had. I wish there were more teachers just like him. Maybe if there were, more kids would stay in school."

I figured that last line would blow Uncle Herm right out of the water.

"If there were more teachers like Retzlaff, we'd all be back in Nazi Germany. Yeah, that would be real good." Uncle Herm walked off before I could answer.

I watched him go. *Probably needs a drink. Hasn't had one for at least fifteen minutes.* I thought about yelling that after him but I knew I'd be in big time crap with my dad if I did.

What had Uncle Herm said — about Mr. R "peddling that garbage for years"? I wondered how he knew anything about Mr. R. One thing was obvious — he didn't know much.

Five

There's some stuff that doesn't excite me like it seems to excite everybody else at school — stuff like grad. There are people who are already talking about our grad night. It's three freaking years away and they're already planning the theme. Should we go with something futuristic like *Guardians of the Galaxy*? Or maybe something about hope, with a giant hope chest on stage? All the grads could pull out something to show the crowd, something to do with hope and life after high school and stuff like that. Yeah, I can hardly wait.

And birthdays. That's another one I can pretty well do without. I guess it's because in my whole life I don't think I ever got what I wanted from my parents on my birthday. When I was little I got clothes instead of racing car models or Hot Wheels stuff. And now that I want clothes, I get stuff that's mostly just embarrassing. Last year it was a 3-D jigsaw puzzle thing of the *Titanic*. Sweet.

So I wasn't expecting any more out of this October 29 than any of the other fifteen October 29s.

Surprise! It was a blast. Jen had a party at her house and we drank a fair amount of beer, ate a fair amount of pizza, and laughed most of the night. Hennie and Big Nose Kate did a hilarious impersonation of me hitting on Patti Bailer at the beach. It got a little raunchy, but I laughed till tears were rolling down my cheeks. We danced some and for a special birthday present, Jen offered to "smash my virginity like a bug." I wasn't sure if she meant it or not, although she probably did since I'm one of the few guys at Parkerville who hasn't spent an evening with the lovely Jen. Anyway, I laughed, turned mega-red (according to T-Ho), and went home with my bug unsmashed.

Oh, and my parents got me a hoodie that was actually fairly cool and a pair of Adidas that had to involve some serious coin. I loved turning sixteen.

And the biggest deal about this birthday was that it meant getting my licence and finally getting behind the wheel of the Biscayne and, who knows, maybe even taking out Patti Bailer.

NOVEMBER

One

Which is pretty much what happened. The driving test was a walk in the park. I'd been driving since I was fourteen and I'd aced driver's ed at school. I nailed the exam the first time — even the parallel parking.

And the date — my first with Patti Bailer — went okay too. Started with a movie — Adam Sandler, good for some first-date laughs — then it was pizza and telling each other our life stories and the midnight drive back to Patti's place, which was in the country. Her parents had bought this acreage about thirty kilometres out of town.

I think she liked the Biscayne. And I think she liked me. When we got to her place, it was all big smiles and a pretty spectacular goodnight kiss. I drove off feeling like I'd won the Daytona 500. The victory lap lasted about five of the twenty minutes back to town. I took a different route home and it wasn't long before I realized it wasn't my best move.

First there was the smell. There's a dairy a few miles out of town. It's not anybody's favourite place to go or even pass by. There's supposed to be like four thousand cows that get milked there — it's one of the area's biggest businesses. The dairy is called Snow White — cute. The problem isn't the milk. It's the fact that four thousand cows produce four thousand regular contributions of cowshit. There are lagoons at the dairy where I guess the shit and urine go — it sure smells like it, and every time you drive by *someone* in the car says, "I am so glad I don't live within breathing distance of this place." Or something similar.

I survived Snow White, mostly by holding my breath. But not long after I passed the dairy and actually started breathing again, I passed some guys going the other way in a Ford pickup. The driver gave me the finger and turned his lights out right after he passed me, I guess to freak me out if I looked in the rear-view mirror. Which I did. That's when the *pop, hiss, whoppa-whoppa-whoppa* noise and the way the Biscayne wanted to pull to the right told me I had a blow-out ... the slow kind, not the dangerous jerk-you-into-the-ditch kind.

I let the car slow down on its own (don't brake with a blowout — *Driver's Ed Manual*) and coasted to a stop as far over on the shoulder as I could get. I found the flashlight in the glove box, got out, and had a look. Right rear, flatter than a DVD.

I was okay with it. "Could have been worse," I said to no one. I talk to myself sometimes and in the dark, a long way from town with a flat tire, talking to myself seemed like a good idea.

"It could have happened before I got Patti home. Then there would have been the pissed-off dad to deal with when we got back late. Or it could have happened just *before* the guys in the Ford pickup went by. So this is fine, this is cool."

And it was. Until I opened the trunk of the car. There was an empty space where the spare tire should have been. I said, "Shit." I might've said it a couple of times.

I'd taken the tire out when I was vacuuming the car for The Big Date (yeah, like Patti was going to look in the trunk) and I'd forgotten to put it back in. (Don't drive without a spare — *Driver's Ed Manual*).

No big deal, right? It's for moments like this that God invented cell phones. A quick call home and problem solved. And that's exactly what I would have done if my cell phone had had any juice in it. Deader than a Christmas turkey. Car charger? At home.

Perfect.

I had a decision to make. It was too late to be pounding on some farmer's door and there was no way I was going back to Patti's to wake up her parents. That meant I had to walk or try to hitch a ride. If I started walking, that would finish the hitchhiking idea. No one would pick up a kid walking along a deserted highway after midnight. They *might* pick up someone standing beside an obvious breakdown. *If* anyone actually came along. And if they believed it *was* a breakdown.

Or I could just walk and forget trying to get a ride. It was maybe fifteen minutes back to town by car. *By car travelling at highway speed*. That meant at least an hour of walking then another ten minutes or so after

I got to town because we lived on the far side — by the school. Hour, maybe hour and a half total. Pitch black, no moon. Lots of stars, but they weren't giving off much light.

So what was the deal? Was I afraid of the dark? No, not afraid ... a little nervous was all. I looked up at the Big Dipper. "What about the Biscayne? I hate to leave it out here for very long and who knows if the ol' man will get out of bed and drive me back here ... especially when he hears about me forgetting the spare."

Now I'm talking to the stars. Perfect. *Talk to the Stars*. Not a bad name for a reality show. Or maybe our grad.

I shone the flashlight around looking for ... what? Bloodthirsty wolves that just happened to have come down out of the hills and were hoping someone would break down at this very spot? Or maybe escaped convicts. Yeah, all of them doing life for multiple murders and all of 'em packing.

No wolves. No killer convicts. But there was something. My light had picked up something in the field. Too far away to really see, but it felt familiar ... like I'd been there before or knew the place or something. I crossed the ditch and went up to the barbed wire fence. I waited for a minute or so, then looked up and down the highway to make sure I wouldn't miss a chance for a ride while I explored. *If* I explored.

And don't ask me why I wanted to, because I don't know. It's not like I was drawn to the place by some strange irresistible extraterrestrial force. Actually, about 70 percent of my brain cells were opposed to me walking out there. And a few were screaming "asshole" inside my head.

Anyway, I went. End of story.

But not right away. I waited a few more seconds then worked my way through the barbed wire and out into the field. I hadn't gone ten steps before I stepped in a hole and twisted my ankle. Not bad, just enough to give me an excuse to swear. My voice seemed extra loud.

I decided it would be best to shine the light a little closer to where I was walking instead of off in the distance. I walked slower. And for quite a while. And I was right. I had been here before. I saw the shadows of the round bales that were still in exactly the same place they'd been the last time I'd walked in this field. I figured *okay, just a little farther then I'm out of here.*

There it was. The foundation we'd seen after the beach volleyball game. That plant, what had T-Ho called it? Bidmore. Bid-something.

He'd said people had died here, I'd forgotten how many. I looked around for a while longer, turning in a circle with the flashlight out in front of me. I hadn't really looked at the foundation all that carefully the last time but I looked at it now. First thing I noticed — this plant must have been huge. The foundation I was standing next to stretched off into the distance until it was out of the range of my flashlight. Not all the foundation was there, of course — it had crumbled away in places — but I could get a feel for the place just the same.

I walked until I could see where the foundation met another wall that went off to the right at a ninety-degree angle. I tried to imagine what the place had looked like when it was still standing. Before it exploded.

Some people died. Right here. That's what T-Ho had told us.

I shivered.

Yeah, if T-Ho had wanted to do the scary ghost thing, he should have waited for night. I'm not a ghost guy, but I swear to god it felt colder, and quieter, right at that moment in the ruins of that old plant. I remembered the first time I'd been there, with The Six, thinking how great it would have been if there hadn't been any noise. I'd wanted quiet. And now I had it. I shivered again, looked over my shoulder then started back to the car.

I hadn't gone more than three feet when I felt something under my foot. Something soft. My first thought was animal. Like I'd maybe stepped on a little furry something or other. I stepped back and aimed my light at the ground. It was soft all right, even *looked* a little like an animal. But it wasn't an animal at all. It was a toque. The black, tight-fitting kind that some guys wear. That Rebel wore. Every day, 24/7, 365.

I picked it up and stuffed it in the front of my jacket. I'm not sure why. I told myself I'd return it to Rebel next time I saw him. But I knew I wouldn't really. Because I'd have to tell him where I'd found it. And for some reason I didn't think I'd be doing that.

I kept walking. When I got to the Biscayne, I looked up and down the highway one more time. *Okay, that's it … there isn't a car within five hundred miles. My ankle's fine. I'm gonna walk.*

I walked ... for maybe fifteen minutes. So far nothing had leaped out of the ditch to eat me. No alien spacecraft had swooped down to take me prisoner so I could write an article for one of those magazines they keep right by the counter at the grocery store.

But a vehicle was coming. Another decision to make. Do I try to hitch a ride? Do I get in the car with some stranger at one in the morning? And what if it's the flippin-the-bird boys in the pickup? I looked back and saw the headlights. Couldn't tell if it was a car or truck. As it got closer I was pretty sure it was a car. I turned and kept walking. I was still making up my mind as the car roared by, then slowed down, stopped, backed up, and stopped alongside me. By then I'd decided that nothing would get me in that car. I had my head down and was walking like I had someplace important to get to.

"Andy? Andy Crockett?"

A drug-crazed killer who wanted to strangle me and leave my bones for the coyotes wouldn't know my name, would he? Besides, this wasn't a he. The voice belonged to a woman. I looked over at the car.

Mrs. Ellis! And Mr. Ellis driving. Yes!

The Ellis's live a couple of blocks from my house. I passed their house most days when I walked to school. When they offered a lift I was in the car before Mrs. Ellis could say, "The back door's unlocked."

"Great to see you guys," I said and meant it.

"Was that your car back there?" Mr. Ellis looked at me in the rear-view mirror.

"Yes, sir. Flat tire. My dad has the spare at home.

I guess he forgot to put it back." I wasn't sure why I lied. I guess I didn't want them to think *oh, another stupid teenager.*

"It's late for you to be out here, Andy," Mrs. Ellis swung around to look at me, which wasn't easy since she was what those ads call a full-figured woman. A *full*-figured woman.

"I was just driving a friend home." I didn't feel like telling her any more than that.

She looked at me for a while like she was trying to figure out the real truth about my being on the road at that hour. Or maybe she was just stuck and couldn't get around to face the front again.

Then she inhaled like she was going to say something, but she didn't. She finally got turned around but she kept looking over at Mr. Ellis like she wanted him to pick up on this line of questioning. Mr. Ellis yawned. We got to the edge of town and I have to admit I was glad to see lights again. Although most of the houses were dark ... including mine. Mr. Ellis stopped the car in front of our driveway.

"Thanks, Mr. and Mrs. Ellis. I really appreciate the ride," I smiled at their backs. Mrs. Ellis turned her head about a quarter turn and Mr Ellis grunted. I got out of the car, completely unaware that for the next few hours my life was going to be like a bad sitcom.

Two

I watched and waved as Mr. and Mrs. Ellis drove off—
I thought it was the polite thing to do after getting a
ride home. Then I turned and started up the driveway.
Dad's Dodge pickup was where it always was — on
the right side of the driveway. Mom's Accord must
have been in the garage. As I walked passed the truck,
I noticed a shape in the middle of the front seat. A
human shape.

I knew whose shape it was. And why it was there.
Uncle Herm had gotten pissed again and was sleeping
it off out here. His chin was slumped down onto his
chest and he was out like a light. He'd done this a few
times. The Dodge was a one-ton dually with an auto-
matic, so he could sit in the middle without having a
stick shift jabbed between his legs. I figured leaning
against the window would be more comfortable but I
guess if you're drunk when you climb into the truck,
maybe comfort isn't a big deal.

I thought about trying to wake him up, but Uncle
Herm was a large man — very large — and getting

a drunk, a big one, out of the front seat of a pickup truck and into the house wouldn't be easy.

I opened the front door of the house and turned on the living room light. Stepping out of my shoes, I sock-footed my way to my parents' room at the far end of the hall. I pushed open the door and whispered, "Dad," hoping somehow to wake him up without waking Mom. It didn't work.

"Andy? What time is it?"

"It's about one, Mom," I answered. "I need Dad to drive me back to my car. I had a flat and the spare is in the garage."

I heard Dad grunt and mumble. I didn't get all of it but I was able to make out "not now" and "morning."

"I don't want to leave the Biscayne out on the high-way all night." I pushed the door open a little further so I could see them. "There are a lot of nuts around. It won't take long."

"Yes, there are a lot of nuts around," my dad said. He was wide awake now, but he hadn't moved except to pull the covers up a little further. It wasn't going well.

"Sorry, Dad."

"Why don't you get the spare out of the garage and roll it back to the car and change it yourself?"

I knew he wasn't serious. But even if he had been I didn't have to answer that one.

"Larry, he can't do that! He could be out all night." Mom sat up in bed. "You better go with him."

"I was going to," Dad grumbled. "I just wanted him to feel like crap first. Sort of like I feel right now."

"Sorry, Dad," I said again.

"I'll get dressed and meet you outside."

I closed the bedroom door softly and headed for the garage. By the time Dad got outside I had the spare in the back of the pickup and was standing by the passenger side.

"Uncle Herm's in there." I nodded in the direction of my uncle's huge form, which as near as I could tell, hadn't moved since I'd first seen him. "What are we going to do with him?"

"Nothing," Dad said. "The man's dead to the world. You get on one side, I get on the other. That way he doesn't tip over."

Like bookends. "Okay." I got in the truck. Dad fired it up, backed onto the street, and we took off without letting the diesel engine warm up, something my dad never did. I didn't think it would be a good idea to mention that at this particular time.

As it turned out, Dad wasn't in all that bad a mood. "So, how was the date?"

"Great," I said. "Patti's really nice but she's, uh … "

"What?"

"She's like really smart…, you know?"

"You say that like it's a bad thing."

"No, it's not a bad thing! It's just that I think she's a lot smarter than me."

"Actually, I doubt that," Dad said. "You're quite a bit more intelligent than you let on. But even if she was, so what?"

It was a weird conversation since we couldn't see each other unless we both leaned really far forward and looked past Uncle Herm.

"Yeah, I guess."

As we drove through town I explained to Dad where I'd gotten the flat. I kept an eye out for the guys in the pickup. No sign of them. Once we got out on the highway, I figured I owed it to him to say something a dad might like to hear in the middle of the night.

"I'm doing pretty good in social."

"Is that the class what's-his-name teaches?"

"Mr. Retzlaff."

"He still teach that stuff about the Holocaust?"

First Uncle Herm and now Dad. I wondered if they'd been talking to each other. "Uh … well, we just started the unit on the war and stuff." Which wasn't true. We were pretty far into it. I didn't really want to talk about Mr. Retzlaff with my dad, though. Especially if he was on the same page as Uncle Herm.

"Your brother told me about it when he had him for social. He said he liked the guy though."

Though.

"When Tim tore up his knee playing football, Retzlaff came to the house a couple of times. Seemed all right."

Seemed.

"Some of the parents were pretty upset with his teaching a couple of years ago. Had a meeting with the principal or the school board or something. Nothing came of it as far as I know. But —"

"There's the car." I was glad we were there and could end the current conversation. I felt like I was betraying Mr. R or something, listening to all this stuff about him.

I mean, there was part of me that sort of wanted to know more. But the other part of me wanted to be loyal to the best teacher I'd ever had. Anyway, we were at the car so that was the end of the Retzlaff talk.

Dad pulled the pickup around in a U-turn so his lights would be on the rear of the Biscayne. We got out and he stepped around to the back box of the pickup. He reached in and pulled my spare up and out. Then he threw it back in and looked at me.

"What?"

"Did you feel that tire when you put it in the truck?"

I shook my head. "No. Should I have?"

"Wouldn't've been a bad idea. It's just as flat as the one on that car."

"Shit." I didn't swear much in front of my parents but it seemed appropriate just then.

Dad must have thought so too. He started to laugh. So I laughed with him.

"What do we do now?"

"Two choices are all we've got." Dad shrugged his shoulders. His shadow looked huge behind the light from the headlights. "We can give up and go home and explain all this to your mom…, or we go to town and wake up Jake Bannering at the tire shop and get him to fix it. Your mom's going to think we're both nuts. Besides, I promised her I'd get this handled for you, so I say we go with Bannering … "

"At two o'clock in the morning?"

"At two o'clock in the morning," Dad nodded. "One of the joys of small town living. You try this in the city, might get you shot."

And that was the last word said until we pulled up in front of Jake's Tire Store on Main Street.

Main Street has only two streetlights on it, but one of them isn't far from the tire shop. So there was a fair amount of light where we parked. Mr. Bannering's place was a Texaco gas station a long time ago. I knew that because you can still see the faded letters — T-e-x-a-c — up high on the wall that faces the street. The house was attached to the side of the shop and looked like it was pretty old too. The yard must have been the storage area for anything that wasn't needed anymore in the tire shop. Lots of rims were scattered here and there on the lawn along with some ratty-looking tires, a few tools, some five-gallon pails, and a bunch of stuff that was pretty much garbage.

"I'll go and wake up Jake." Dad turned off the truck and climbed out of the cab. I was left alone with Uncle Herm, still hunched over all large and … quiet.

Quiet. Strangely quiet. Why wasn't Uncle Herm snoring? Or at least breathing that loud drunk breathing he was so good at?

I looked at him. It was the first time I'd looked really closely at him since our journey had begun. I bent over and put my ear as close to his mouth as I could get. I expected a not-great smell.

Nothing.

At least I thought nothing. The passenger door opened and I jumped, hitting my head on the roof of the cab.

"Surprised you, huh?" Dad laughed.

Yeah, major funny, Dad.

"Bannering will be here in a minute. He was all right with me getting him up but Mrs. B wasn't real happy…. I think we're off her Christmas-card list."

"Dad … I … I think there might be something wrong with Uncle Herm."

"I know there's something wrong with Uncle Herm. There'll be a hell of a lot more wrong with him tomorrow."

"No, I mean something really wrong. He's not moving at all. I don't think he's breathing. Maybe he's … "

Dad looked at his brother then at me. "Naw." He went around to the driver's side, opened the door, and leaned in. He stared at Uncle Herm for a few seconds then lifted one of my uncle's large arms and let it fall. It came down in a hurry and made a thump on the seat. Finally Dad twisted around so he could see Uncle Herm's face.

Then he straightened up, kind of herky-jerky. He didn't say anything for what seemed like a really long time. "Andy … I think your uncle's … dead."

I looked at Dad and at Uncle Herm "You *think*? You can't tell for sure?"

"Well, hell, I mean, yeah I can tell … he's … he's dead."

We stood there looking at each other and trying to think of what to say next. This wasn't one of those life situations you get much practice dealing with. Dad closed the door and walked to the front of the pickup. I got out of the truck and backed my way to a place right next to Dad. Actually pretty close to him.

Mr. Bannering came shuffling out to the truck. He had his coveralls on but was still in his bedroom slippers.

"Get the tire into the shop and let's get this over with," he ordered.

"Uh … Jake," my dad looked at him, "I need you to do something for me…. You had much experience with … the dead?"

"What the hell are you — ?"

"Dead people. Could you recognize one, y'know … if you saw him?"

"Tires, I fix tires, and I don't feel like having some stupid philosophical discussion in the middle of the damn street in the middle of the damn night. Now are you gonna get that tire into —"

Dad raised his voice. "I'm talking about dead people here. We think Herm might be … gone."

"Gone?"

"Yeah … gone. Dead, for Christ's sake."

"It's coming on to two in the morning and if you think this is funny, I got —"

I'd been listening to my dad and I didn't think he sounded like he was kidding around. "We're serious, Mr. Bannering," I said. "Uncle Herm — he's in there and he's not moving or breathing or anything."

Mr. Bannering looked at me like suddenly there was something to this. Like having me say it instead of Dad — that seemed to get his attention. Big time.

He leaned into the cab of the truck and did pretty much the same thing Dad had done a few minutes before. Then he stepped back. And stepped back again.

"If the boy wasn't here, I'd be sayin' some words I won't say *with* him here."

"Yeah," Dad said.

Mr. Bannering lifted a big hand and rubbed it across his face a couple of times. "Let me get this straight. You're driving around the country getting tires fixed and who knows what all else with a dead body in the truck. And you've got the boy with you. Are you some kind of psycho?"

I could see Mr. Bannering was upset. Or maybe disgusted is a better word.

"We didn't know he was dead, Jake," Dad shook his head. "I swear to god we just found out —"

"Well, now you know, so get him out of here and off Main Street." He stood and watched us as if he wanted to make sure we did what he said.

Nobody moved. I guess I was waiting for Dad. He had his arms crossed and he was thinking. "Jake, wait a second." It seemed like Dad was shouting, but maybe that was just because it was so quiet on the street.

Mr. Bannering turned around. "What?"

"You might as well fix the tire."

"What?"

"Look, we're here anyway. It won't make any difference to Herm and the tire needs fixing."

It sounded kind of insensitive the way Dad said it, but I kind of agreed with him. Especially since I was still worried about my car out there on the highway.

"Well, shouldn't we at least send for an ambulance?"

Dad thought about that. "Be forever getting here. And it'll cost. We'll drop him off."

Mr Bannering seemed to think that made at least *a little* sense.

"After you change the tire."

"The. Man. Is. Dead." Mr. Bannering said it with a pause between each word.

"I know that and I wish he wasn't, I really do. He's my brother. But we're here and we have to get Andy's car off the highway and we need this tire."

"I can't believe this whole deal. This is so ridiculous I can't even —"

"Just fix the damn tire, Jake."

Mr. Bannering hesitated. "All right, bring it inside … away from … that." He waved in the direction of the pickup. "And I'm charging you double."

Dad looked at me, shook his head and took the tire inside the shop. While they were inside I walked up and down the block hoping no one would be out at this hour who might just happen to walk by the truck. And even more I hoped that Patti Bailer would never find out how I'd spent the hours immediately after our first date.

When Dad came out of the tire shop rolling the tire in front of him, I prayed that the weird part of the night was just about over. It wasn't.

We started driving. I looked back and saw Mr. Bannering standing on the sidewalk watching us. His lips were moving and whatever he was telling himself I bet it wasn't what a nice, normal family the Crocketts were. I couldn't really blame him.

I just wanted to get out on the highway as quickly as possible so we could get back and be done with the whole thing. Dad had other ideas. Our next stop was the hospital. Dad parked at the emergency entrance, right behind the town's ambulance. It's weird the stuff that goes through your mind at certain times. I remember thinking that this night had convinced me that ambulance driver was one career they couldn't pay me enough money to do.

Dad went through the double glass doors of the emergency entrance and I stayed in the truck, careful not to look over at my dead uncle. After a few minutes a nurse came out and for about the twentieth time that night somebody checked out my uncle.

Apparently just *telling* people someone is dead isn't good enough.

The nurse looked at Uncle Herm for a while, did the pulse thing and stuff again, then looked at my dad. She nodded and said, "I'm sorry but he … your brother … has definitely passed away."

Dad nodded and wiped his sleeve across his mouth. He seemed to be swallowing a lot. I'd never really known how my Dad felt about his alcoholic brother but I could see that, as weird as this whole thing was, it was tough for him.

"What do we do?" he asked the nurse.

"You have two choices. You can leave him here — there's a morgue in the basement — or you can take him to the funeral home yourself. Seeing as it's so late you may want to leave him —"

"We'll take him … to the funeral home … uh … thanks." Dad shook hands with the nurse, which I thought was kind of strange, but *everything* about this night had been strange.

89

The nurse walked off into the hospital and Dad got back in the truck. "I hate the word 'morgue,'" Dad shoved the key in the ignition like he was punching somebody in the gut.

I was pretty much convinced that this was never going to end. Plus I was really tired. But resting my head against the side window and trying to get a little sleep, sitting next to Uncle Herm — that wasn't going to happen. As we drove to Stan Marley's Funeral Home — it was also where Mr. Marley lived, which is a little creepy if you ask me — I noticed that the Christmas decorations were up on the power poles on Main Street. They weren't lit yet but they were up and ready to go. That meant that in the next few days Mom would say, "The town yuletide decorations look lovely this year." She said it every year. Funny I should remember her words just then. Maybe it was because my mom is the only real person I know who says "yuletide," or maybe it was because the decorations are the same every year.

I snuck another peek at Uncle Herm. I wondered what he'd think if he knew I was focused on Christmas decorations while he was sitting there all dead in the truck. I decided to stare at the glove box instead. More appropriate.

We didn't get an answer to all our pounding on the door and ringing the bell at the funeral home. I guess it was foolish to think that something might actually go right on the night from hell. Standing on the steps looking at the plaque on the door that said "Welcome," Dad shook his head then looked at me. I couldn't tell what he was thinking. But I had a feeling that he wasn't real happy with me just then.

"I don't think Uncle Herm died because I had a flat tire." I told him.

He nodded his head and closed his eyes for a few seconds. I figured maybe the stress and lack of sleep was getting to him too.

He opened his eyes. "Probably not," was all he said.

He looked back at the door to the funeral home. "We might as well go put the tire on the car and we'll decide what to do with Herm after that." Dad's voice didn't have much bounce in it, another sign that the night was taking a toll on the guy.

"It's okay, Dad, we can leave it," I told him. "What the hell, it's almost morning anyway."

Dad didn't laugh or even smile. "Andy, we're going to put that goddamn tire on that car. Let's go."

The way Dad said it meant that an argument wouldn't be welcome. So I spent another fifteen minutes sitting next to my dead uncle — it was creeping me out way worse now that I *knew* he was dead.

It was a lot cooler than it had been the first time or even the second time I'd stood beside the Biscayne that night. But I was out there handing the lug nuts to Dad and trying to look like I was helping. Anything to keep from being in the truck.

I looked up and thought about how great the stars looked and then felt real guilty for noticing nice things like stars and Christmas decorations. Orion was up there, all warrior-like with the three stars in his belt. I bet he never went through anything like this.

When the tire was changed Dad said, "I'll go back to town and see if I can raise Marley. You get home to bed."

Those were the first words I'd heard in a couple of hours that made any sense at all. I was in the Biscayne and out of there before Dad could change his mind. And that's how it ended.

For me. The next morning Dad told me Mr. Marley had finally come to the door and the two of them had wheeled Uncle Herm into the funeral home.

The funeral was three days later. I was actually feeling bad about Uncle Herm and it was a sad funeral, too — I guess most of them are. But every time I thought about driving around the countryside most of the night with a dead person in the pickup so we could change a tire, I had to work a little at not laughing right there in the middle of the funeral.

The Six all came to the funeral, I'm not sure why. I didn't think they'd ever met Uncle Herm, but I suppose they might have seen him during one of his nights out. But I was pretty sure they were there just so they could *say* they'd been there. Like thirty years later when people were still talking about the weirdest flat-tire changing that had ever taken place in Parkerville history, everyone would want to be able to say, "I was at the funeral, you know."

And they were hell on the sandwiches at the after-burial tea they had in the church basement. Hennie took a whole tray and pretended to be passing them around but I noticed that if anybody actually reached for a sandwich, he'd turn away before they could make contact. I'm guessing The Six downed pretty well that whole tray.

Three

Mr. R was walking up and down between the rows of desks, a battered old hard copy of a *Webster's* dictionary in his hands.

"The word hoax is defined as 'something intended to deceive; deliberate trickery intended to gain an advantage.'" Mr. Retzlaff wrote the definition on the board then underlined the word "deceive."

"Who can give me an example?"

No one put up their hand so I did.

"Alamo."

"What about all those Elvis sightings? I mean, the guy's dead."

Somebody at the back of the room said, "Andy's an expert on dead people." I couldn't tell for sure who it was, but it sounded like Hennie. The whole class laughed. Yeah, it had taken about twenty minutes for the Uncle Herm story to make it through the halls of Parkerville Comp. Which made me the school dufus. So now, not only were people not talking to me — they were laughing as they walked past. Nice.

And there were the inevitable comments from The Six:

— T-Ho: Hey, Alamo, can I catch a ride home after school? Of course I can't, I'm not dead.

— Jen: No wonder we call you Alamo. Weren't there a lot of dead bodies then too?

— Hennie: Hey man, how unpopular do you have to be you got to go ridin' with dead folks?

— Lou: You couldn't get anybody else to help you change a tire?

Big Nose Kate didn't say anything, although she laughed more than any of them and Rebel just shook his head every time he saw me.

I was sure Mr. R had to have heard about Uncle Herm, but he didn't say anything about it.

"Not bad," he nodded. "Those sightings are definitely intended to deceive, although I'm not sure how telling someone you saw Elvis at Home Depot buying plumbing fixtures could gain anyone an advantage."

Everyone laughed again. Everyone but me. I didn't feel much like laughing.

"But it's still a good example." Mr. Retzlaff changed directions and started walking up and down in front of the class. "So not all hoaxes are bad. But some are. Some are *very* bad. I want to talk about one of the worst today."

He had our attention like he usually did. "We talked last week about the Holocaust and the discussion got around to the pictures. I'm sure many of us have seen pictures of the concentration camps."

A few people nodded. I'd never seen the pictures he was talking about, but I nodded too.

"I told you a few classes back that we would come back to the subject of pictures." Mr. R set the dictionary down on the table next to his desk. "Pictures … pictures … pictures. They're worth a thousand words, isn't that the expression?"

The whole time I'd been watching Mr. R, he'd been reminding of someone. I finally figured it out. It wasn't one particular someone. It was a bunch of someones. Lawyers. The ones you see on TV shows when they're in courtrooms and they're convincing the jury of something. I figured Mr. R could have been a good lawyer.

He went to his computer. Mr. R had one of those set-ups where he could punch stuff into his computer and it showed up on the smart board at the front of the classroom.

"Pictures," he said again.

He started tapping at the computer keys. A picture of a bus came up on the screen. It was green, a passenger bus like you'd see in the big cities. It was travelling on a busy street, right toward the camera. Then there was another picture on the screen. This time it was Mr. R in shorts and a T-shirt. He looked like he was on holidays. His hair was pretty long and he was wearing sunglasses. He was staring at the camera and smiling. It looked like he was in a parking lot — a ball park or some kind of stadium behind him, but off a ways.

Some of us laughed. Mr. R did too. "That's my pre-makeover look."

Then Mr. R put a third picture up on the screen. He was still standing there smiling, but now he was in the middle of the street and another bus, or maybe the same one, was right behind him — coming right at him.

"Boy, that's gonna hurt." Mr. R turned away from the computer and looked at us. He had the same smile on his face as the one in the picture. We laughed again. Harder this time.

"Now is there anybody here who thinks I was hit by that bus?"

Nobody raised a hand.

"Interesting." Mr. R went back to the computer and hit the keys again.

Everyone in the class either gasped or groaned. A couple of people yelled, "Eeoo, gross."

Which it was.

The picture was of Mr. R lying on the pavement covered in blood and looking pretty much dead. It was *definitely* gross.

"Well, I guess you're all wrong. Obviously I *was* hit by that bus. And it *did* hurt."

There was silence in the room for a few minutes after that. Then one more picture — Mr. R standing looking at the camera with all the blood and goo still all over him. He was holding a little sign up to the camera. It read, "Gotcha."

The laughing was probably louder than it needed to be. I guess we didn't know what to think.

"Pictures. Can we trust them? Or can they be made to tell a story that's quite different from what really happened?"

He spent the next few minutes showing us pictures that were all hoaxes. One was of this person smiling into a camera from the observation deck of the World Trade Center. In the background was an airliner coming right at the building. I remembered that picture and how it had been in newspapers and on the internet and stuff right after 9/11. There were lots more pictures that did the same kind of thing. And some stuff from that old *Forrest Gump* movie — the Tom Hanks' character with presidents and other famous people. There was even a hilarious picture of Britney Spears' face on the body of a woman who must have weighed four hundred pounds. Hennie yelled out, "I thought these were supposed to be hoax pictures." Everyone, even Mr. R laughed at that.

But then it wasn't funny. There were pictures of mounds of dead bodies — men and women, naked and piled in huge pits. Then these horribly skinny people, all of them bald and all of them looking like they were close to being dead. People looking out of the doors of train cars — cattle cars, I think, but these weren't cattle, they were people and they looked scared. Lots of them were little kids and some were crying and reaching out, like they were trying to say something to the person holding the camera.

And though I'd never seen them before I knew these were Holocaust pictures. And they *were* horrible.

No action movie I'd ever seen, with mangled, bloody bodies all over the place, could match the grainy, black-and-white pictures we were looking at.

Then it was over. Mr. R didn't say anything, he just let the blank screen and the soft whirring sound of the computer be the only things that were happening in the room.

Then in a very soft voice he said, "Horrific images. The worst. And not one person in this room can help but hate those responsible for what happened to the people in the pictures."

He took two steps toward us and leaned forward. "*If* they are real. *If* they are true. *If* they are to be believed."

For a few seconds more Mr. R didn't say anything at all. The place was as quiet as any classroom I've been in since naptime in kindergarden.

Mr. R shut off the computer and stood facing us. "Your assignment," he was using his normal voice again, regular volume. And he was smiling. "Devise a hoax. It can be anything you want. It can even be your take on an existing hoax. But it has to be designed to deceive people, in this case your classmates and me, and you have to provide ways … methods that you would use to sell people on your hoax. Due in two weeks. Everyone will stand up in front of the class and sell their hoax to the rest of us poor unsuspecting lambs. We'll start on Friday the 29th and take as many classes as are needed to hear everyone's presentation. I'm thinking about five minutes per presentation. Much longer than that and it's like an awards show.

The bastards start playing the music and you get run off the stage."

The bell rang and we tumbled out into the hall, everybody laughing and loudly promising to "suck in the rest of you."

Another amazing class with Mr. R.

Four

I'd been walking to math class — and listening to dead guy comments — when Mr. R came around the corner.

"Ah, Mr. Crockett. The very person I was hoping to see."

My first thought was that I must have done crappy on an assignment and was about to hear about it. Except that we hadn't had any assignments recently.

"Would you have a few minutes after school? I'd like to talk to you. It won't take long."

"Uh sure … I guess so."

"Good, just come to my classroom after last class. And Alamo …"

I'd started to walk away but I stopped and looked back at him. He was smiling.

"Don't let it get to you. They'll let up on the dead guy stuff in a couple of days."

I nodded even though I wasn't sure I believed him, and wandered off in the direction of math class.

After school I was at Mr. R's door as the last students were coming out of the room shrugging into coats and backpacks as they walked. Mr. R was sitting at his desk, writing something. I stayed at the door.

"Uh, Mr. R? You wanted to see me?"

He looked up. "Come in."

I walked in and stood in front of his desk waiting for him to finish what he was doing.

Mr. R set his pen down, looked at me foe a few seconds before he said, "Sit down, Alamo."

I sat in the first desk of the row in front of Mr. R. I looked down at the surface of the desk. There was the usual graffiti: *Physics Sucks, Danielle J is a slut, G.M. loves G.M.* (I thought that one was a bit weird.)

Mr. R stood up, came around the front of his desk, moved some papers, and sat on the edge. He wasn't smiling but he didn't look pissed off either.

"I told you that one day I'd like to talk further about your loss in the wrestling regionals."

I'd kind of forgotten he'd said that. But I nodded. "I should've won."

"Yes, you should have. That was a missed opportunity."

He didn't say anything more for a minute and I tried to figure out what he meant. I mean, sure I would have liked to win for me and for my school. Was that the opportunity I'd missed?

"Do you remember the name of the boy you lost to?" Mr. R made the word "lost" sound like it was the worst thing anyone could do.

I thought. "Uh ... Epstein ... Julius Epstein, I think."

"You think. I know. It *was* Epstein. We don't lose to those people, Andy."

For the first time I wasn't Alamo, I was Andy.

"Yes, sir," I said. To be honest, I didn't know what I was supposed to say. Or what exactly he was talking about.

"The good thing is that there may be another opportunity coming up ... a chance to redeem yourself and to strike back at all that they stand for."

The whole conversation was starting to feel weird. And I still wasn't getting it. I tried to make my face look like everything was making perfect sense to me.

"I've spoken to a couple of other people about the need to stand tall against the influence ... the evil." When he said "evil" he leaned forward and the word was a curse word, no other way to describe it. "And I'm speaking to you now because I have a good feeling about you — that you're a team player. That I ... that *we* all can count on you when the time is right. It's important that you don't miss *this* opportunity."

I nodded.

"Thanks for stopping by, Alamo *(I was Alamo again)*. I hope I didn't keep you from something important."

"No, sir, you didn't."

He reached out and shook my hand ... and smiled for the first time since he'd sat on the corner of the desk. He stood up, walked back around the desk, and returned to whatever it was he'd been doing. He didn't look up at me again and I knew the conversation was over.

When I got back outside I sat in the Biscayne for quite a while before I turned the ignition key. Trying to put things together. Mr. R hadn't said who or what was evil. But Epstein was Jewish, I knew that. And the whole Holocaust discussion. My private chat with Mr. R fit in with that, didn't it?

Didn't it?

The one thing I was pretty sure about was the "couple of other people" Mr. R had spoken to. It had to be T-Ho and Rebel. In my head, I had a picture of the time I'd seen the three of them after school — talking, laughing. As for what the *opportunity* was, I had no clue. I figured it was something I'd find out later.

When the time was right.

Five

My second date with Patti went okay consider- ing I didn't think there'd *be* a second date after the drive-Uncle-Herm's-corpse-around-the-country- side episode. When girls think you're weird and that you come from an even weirder family, they tend to delete your emails without replying. What made this date especially cool, though, was that it was sort of a surprise.

I'd been thinking about trying out for the foot- ball team in grade eleven so I went to one of their games. The games are always on a Friday night — and this was the last game of the season. It wasn't like the game actually meant anything. Our team was in about the middle of the pack (remember what I said about Parkerville being average?) and we had no hope of a playoff spot. We were playing the top team in the league and pretty much getting our butts handed to us.

But that didn't matter because Patti was at the game with two of her friends — two girls I'd seen at school but didn't really know.

Now all I had to do was get her away from the two friends and I'd be in business. My attempt to talk to Patti didn't start well. The first thing out of one of the friend's mouth was, "I don't know about dating this guy, Patti. You could like, die right there in the car or something."

The good thing was Patti didn't laugh. The even better thing was that her two pals had boyfriends on the team and when I suggested that I could take Patti home the two friends were all, like, yeah that would be so nice of you. No dead jokes then, not when they needed me to help them ditch the fifth wheel. I wondered what they'd have done if I hadn't been at the game — leave Patti stranded in the bleachers? But who cared — it was Friday night and I was with her.

We went to Dairy Queen.

Patti wasn't a big talker, not at first. Actually, I already knew that. I'd found out the first time I phoned her. There had been a lot of silence on her end of the line. I kept thinking I had to fill the empty space with words so I said some fairly stupid stuff, like giving her this totally graphic description of when my brother got sick from eating bad egg rolls. I bet she was like, *Mom, if that guy ever phones again, tell him I've moved to Bangladesh.*

The next couple of times I phoned her I had some stuff written down in case I needed it. My first list had about six things on it but I stroked off a couple of them just before I phoned her — the play-by-play of replacing the clutch in the Biscayne and a story about Hennie's mom's boob job, which was pretty funny when Hennie told it but I wasn't sure would be as good coming from me.

But then Patti phoned me this one time and we talked (and *she* talked) like we hadn't seen each other in two years. So I was kind of surprised when she went back to being Miss Quiet again in the DQ. But this time it wasn't shyness, which is what I think was the deal with those first phone calls. This time, she looked like she was just really thinking about stuff.

"What?" I said.

"Hmmm … oh, nothing…, I mean, not nothing…, I just…"

I think she would have told me if T-Ho and Rebel hadn't walked in just then.

They came over to our table before they even ordered. T-Ho looked at Patti and then at me. I was mostly looking at Rebel. It was the first time I'd seen him since before I'd had the flat tire on the Biscayne, except for at Uncle Herm's funeral, which didn't really count since I didn't actually talk to any of The Six. Probably because their mouths were full the whole time.

Rebel was wearing his toque — a different one, though; not black, more of a dark green. That meant I'd been right — the one I'd found at the Bidwell Plant site *was* his. I felt in the pocket of my jacket. It was still there.

"Let me guess," T-Ho gave us one of those ah-ha-I-caught-you looks. "You've been *studying* together."

I shook my head. "Mm-mm. Just drove around for a while. Then came here."

"Driving or parking, you stud?" T-Ho grinned at me.

I felt my cheeks suddenly getting very hot. "Driving," I said but I hated the wimpy way my voice sounded when I said it.

Patti nodded like she was thinking T-Ho still didn't believe me.

Which he didn't. "Whatever."

T-Ho and Rebel started for the counter.

"Hey, T-Ho," I called to him and he turned around. Looked at me … waiting. Like I was about to confess that Patti and I had been doing it in the grocery store parking lot.

"That place we stopped that time — the plant that blew up? What was it called again?" I said it to T-Ho but I was watching Rebel. He didn't look like he was paying attention to anything but his food order.

"Bidwell. Bidwell Gas Plant."

"You never told us how you knew about that place."

"Who cares?" T-Ho shrugged. "What does it matter how I know about it?" He turned and walked up to the counter where Rebel was ordering a double-cheeseburger meal.

Patti and I didn't talk much while they were in there. I was hoping they wouldn't decide to join us. I wasn't sure how Patti would take them. Or how they'd take her. I mean, you could hardly find people more different than Patti and The Six. Maybe they'd kind of accept each other. Or maybe they wouldn't.

But it was okay. T-Ho and Rebel were getting takeout. I remembered you couldn't roll down the driver's side window in the Crap Wagon. No going to the drive-through in that car. That's why they'd come inside.

Even with T-Ho and Rebel in the restaurant, it was pretty quiet. There was no one else in the place except for three girls who looked about thirteen and ate like they were five. A lot of talking and chewing and food-spilling and laughing at the same time.

Then T-Ho's order came and he and Rebel started for the door. But just as they were going out, T-Ho stopped and looked over at me.

"Somebody told me about it. Okay?"

"Sure," I kind of waved my burger in his direction. "Okay."

Rebel never looked our way at all. Patti and I talked about school stuff for a while and then I don't know why but I told her about the time The Six and I had stopped at the ruins of the plant.

It was strange — like I'd pressed the Totally Interested switch. She sat up and looked really intensely at me the whole time I was talking.

"Have you ever heard of that place — the Bidwell Plant?" I asked.

She started to shake her head but then she didn't. "Yes, I have. Just recently. I'd never heard about it before that."

"Whoa, that's a wild coincidence," I said. "Did someone tell you about it?"

She nodded.

"Who?"

"Doesn't matter."

And that was it. I could see she didn't want to talk about it anymore and I didn't think a second date (that barely qualified as a real date already) was the time to push her on something.

The rest of the night was all right. It wasn't one of those laugh-a-minute dates, but I just liked being with Patti, even when she was in a quiet mood. When I took her home, things got pretty intense on the physical side, but for once I didn't push that either. I think that was a good call, because Patti seemed a little happier by the time she hopped out of the Biscayne and headed for the house.

On the way home I thought a lot about Patti and a little about Rebel. Actually I thought about his toque. I was sure he'd had it on when we left the Bidwell Plant that first time with T-Ho and everybody, so that meant he must have gone to the ruins another time and somehow left his toque behind. I tossed that back and forth in my mind for a while. And Patti knew about the Bidwell Plant, too. I wondered if there was some connection. But nothing came to me right away and I went back to thinking about Patti.

And me. Together. Like a couple.

Sweet.

Six

It's weird when a teacher in your school dies during the school year. I mean, not that it ever happened before. But there we were on a Thursday morning — everybody standing around the common area all going, "Did you hear about Mr. Saarkahn?" "Isn't it awful?" People were hugging each other and a bunch of the girls were crying. Some kids were getting flowers and other stuff to put by the door of Mr. Saarkahn's room.

The thing is, it all felt a little too television for me. I know that makes me sound like a cold-hearted creep, especially after almost laughing in the middle of Uncle Herm's funeral, but this just seemed wrong. I'd never had him for a teacher but I knew Mr. Saarkahn wasn't real popular in our school. He was East Indian or Pakistani or something and I'd heard kids say he was pretty hard to understand. Some had said really unpleasant things about him or at least about his teaching. Now he'd had a heart attack while he was out jogging and right away there was a shrine happening and people who didn't like the guy when he was alive were some of the loudest mourners.

I'd seen him in the halls and the cafeteria a few times, but I hadn't really thought about him very much at all, which is about how I figured most people in the school were when it came to Mr. Saarkahn. Except the ones who said the nasty stuff and did bad impersonations of his accent.

I mean it *was* sad — he had a wife and a little kid and he wasn't very old — but I just thought the scene in the common room was a little much. To tell the truth, the thing I was really thinking about was how much death there seemed to be around me all of a sudden. I'd gone through most of my life up to that point without thinking about death and dying hardly at all. About the only time I'd ever thought about it was when my grandpa died, and he was really old which made it seem okay. Or when somebody famous, an athlete, or an entertainer or some world leader, died. And those deaths seemed really far away.

But just in the last while there'd been Uncle Herm and now Mr. Saarkahn. And there were the pictures Mr. R had shown us of all the bodies piled up in ditches during the war. But then maybe that didn't count. I mean, had those pictures been real? Didn't matter; they looked real. And it all seemed part of an awful lot of death. I don't know if it scared me or what, but I know I didn't like it.

* * *

My first class that day was social with Mr. R and I was interested to hear what he'd have to say about the death of a teacher.

And what he said was nothing — at least nothing about Mr. Saarkahn.

Mr. R had the lights off and the blinds closed when we went into the room but that was no big deal since he usually did that when he was putting something up on the screen. But that wasn't it. He sat at his desk in the semi-dark looking at us and saying nothing. So then I thought, okay, this is like having the flag at half-mast or something and this was Mr. R's way of paying tribute to a fellow teacher. Wrong again.

After we'd sat looking at him — and around the room at each other — for a few minutes, Mr. R got out of his chair, walked to the computer table he had at the front of the room, and sat on the corner of it.

"I want you to think about the things that make you the angriest." He was speaking in a low voice like he did when he was building up to something dramatic. So I still figured it was about Mr. Saarkahn.

"Whether it's someone who has let you down or lied to you, or something that someone did to you or someone you care about, or maybe it's something bigger — something big that's happening around you that you don't like but can't do anything about. I want you to think about that and to keep that thought in your head."

We all sat and thought for a while. I came up with two things that really pissed me off — one was how

Diana McNair acted whenever she saw me in the halls. She'd stick her finger in her mouth like she was going to gag or she'd point at me and move her lips and the words she was mouthing weren't the kind you tossed out during Sunday roast-beef dinners. Or she'd give me the finger. Nice.

I didn't figure that was exactly what Mr. R had in mind, though, so my second choice was when my dad had promised to take us all to Disneyland, and then didn't. I think I was about eight or nine, and I'd been looking forward to it for months. I'd told all the kids I knew that we were going to Disneyland; my brother was maybe fourteen and he saved up his money and bought all these clothes he thought would make him look cool in California. Even Mom was pretty stoked about the whole thing. And then, bingo, no trip. And not much explanation either. Just some lame "we can't afford it right now" crap.

I think my dad's a pretty good guy and an okay dad and everything, but getting us all pumped about that trip and then taking it away from us is something I guess I'll always hold against him.

I didn't know what Mr. R had in mind but I figured we'd all sit around in the dark and talk about what it was that made each of us really angry. Which was fine as long as it didn't get all touchy-feely. I took psychology for an option in grade nine and there was a lot of that. It was stupid. And fairly useless unless the teacher's goal (the amazing Mrs. Storch, who was like a hundred and had a moustache) was to have a classroom full of giggling students.

I wasn't sure what the whole "angry" thing had to do with social but I knew Mr. R would have something cool going on before it was all over.

I was half right about what was going to happen. I had the sit-around-in-the-dark-and-talk part right. Except we didn't do much talking — not the students, I mean. Mr. R did all the talking, at least at first.

"We've talked about the war, its causes, some of the terrible things that took place during the war, about the politics of war, and of that war in particular. But we haven't talked about the thing about World War II that makes me angriest." He raised his voice on the word "me" and then dropped it way down again when he said "angriest."

"What do people remember about the war? Well, if they had a loved one or someone they knew well who was killed or badly wounded in the fighting, they remember *that*. And they should.

"Or they might remember how difficult it was for the people back home, who had to do amazing things because so many of the men were away fighting. And they should.

"Or they might remember the great speeches of Churchill, or Roosevelt, or Mackenzie King. And they should."

Mr. R waited for a minute or so and then in a much softer voice he said, "Or they might remember something that has come to be called 'the Holocaust'."

There was a long moment of silence and I'm pretty sure every kid in the class noticed, just like I did, that he didn't say "and they should" on that last point.

After a minute or so, Mr. R cleared his throat. "T-Ho, tell me something that makes you angry."

I figured T-Ho would about faint at having to be the first to speak but he hardly even hesitated. "I hate it when people are cowards. I used to play hockey and I'd hate it when a guy would give you a dirty hit and so you'd go after the guy and he wouldn't fight. He'd just turtle. I hate it when somebody turtles … that pisses me … uh … makes me angry."

"Good, T-Ho," Mr. R nodded. "An excellent example and just the kind of thing I wanted to hear about. Rebel, what about you?"

I figured Mr. R had lost it. First T-Ho and then Rebel. No teacher ever asked a question and then got two members of The Six to answer it. Except there was that after school thing with Mr. R and T-Ho and Rebel. Maybe that was setting this up — having them answer in class. Except what would be the point? Mr. R could have had any kid in that room give him an answer. A good answer.

I was still thinking about that when Rebel gave *his* answer.

"People who use their position to take advantage of others. That really bothers me."

What? Had I heard that correctly? This was Rebel, the guy who didn't say much most of the time and *never* said anything in school unless he absolutely had to, and when he did, it was a couple of grunts and a shrug. *That* Rebel had just given a very good answer and he didn't hesitate or stutter … nothing. Spoke like he was the valedictorian.

"Excellent, Rebel, excellent. Patti, how about you?"

Patti hesitated for a few seconds. I wondered if she was feeling like I was. I was trying to figure out if what I was going to say when it was my turn would totally blow.

"I guess I'm angered by the fighting in the Middle East and how so many people — soldiers and civilians — are dying needlessly."

Mr. R smiled a little at Patti, who I noticed didn't smile back. He didn't say anything but looked over at me. "Andy?"

I was Andy again. Damn. It was like I had to keep proving myself to be Alamo to Mr. R. And for some reason — right then — I wanted to be Alamo. It was like I wanted Mr. R to like me as well as he liked T-Ho and Rebel. *Jesus, I wanted to be as popular as T-Ho and Rebel.* Now *that* was a thought I never expected to have.

I stumbled through my story about the cancelled trip to Disneyland, and the further along I got the lamer it sounded to me. By the time I finished, I was sweating.

"Another very good response," Mr. R nodded and I felt like I'd just won an award or something. I don't know why this — talking about something that pissed us off — had made me so nervous when thinking about the hoax presentation was no big deal.

"And I know if I continued around the room, I'd get many more solid, well-thought-out answers. But I know all of you are wondering where this is all going, or if it's just Retzlaff having a meltdown." Some kids laughed at this.

"I want to go back to some of the things we heard about today. The coward, he … turtles, was that what you called it, T-Ho?"

T-Ho nodded.

"And Rebel takes exception with someone using their position to take advantage of others … and Alamo brought up the case of someone lying and causing pain to someone else."

Alamo. Yes! Except I didn't say my dad had lied. But I didn't bother to correct Mr. R. It wasn't that important. What was important was that I was mentioned in the same breath as T-Ho and Rebel. *Awright!*

"It's interesting that my biggest grievance — the thing that has most angered me in my life — has many of those same elements built into it. A cowardly group of people who have throughout history used their position to take advantage and gain power over others; and yes, they often lied and still do to further their cause. And," Mr R looked over at Patti, "just as was the case in Miss Bailer's example, countless thousands — entire generations of people virtually throughout the civilized world — have suffered because of these people's endless quest to dominate and to take more and more control of the entire globe."

Mr. R went over to his computer and started punching keys.

What came up on the screen was one word — Judaism.

"The Jews. One of the world's most important groups of people, right? Some would have you believe that they are a religious group. But, in fact, they're much more."

118

Mr. R tapped a key. A picture appeared on the screen. Buildings, big buildings. A caption below the picture read Wall Street. "Throughout history, this is a people who have controlled much of the world's finances, making the Jews a powerful force on the globe — some would say more powerful than either their numbers or the nature of their culture deserve."

He tapped again. "And throughout history, the Jew has played one significant card over and over. The we-are-the-oppressed card; the we-are-the-victim card. The people who put Jesus Christ to death, and *they* are the oppressed. A convenient reconstruction of history. And effective. If I can convince all of you that I have historically been dealt with unfairly, even cruelly, then there is a very real chance that decent people, wanting to do the right thing, will turn a blind eye to what I am all about. And if what I'm about is gaining global domination by controlling the finances of the world, well perhaps even that will be allowed to happen. And if, along the way, someone steps forward and says very forcefully, 'No! I won't let you play that card, not any more, not here and not now,' then that person is branded intolerant, a racist, a bigot … someone who hates, and hating is always wrong. But sometimes there are people, even nations, that will make a stand even though they face becoming the bad guys of world public opinion. They make that very unpopular stand because they believe it is the right thing to do. And they have the courage to do it.

"So we have a leader and his people, a country in this case, who had faced the unfairness of the Treaty of

Versailles — you all remember that? They were bearing a justifiable ill-will toward much of the world — we agreed on that, right? So, you have this country feeling, as T-Ho felt in this very classroom, that it was time to fight back. That same leader and his people were also willing to make an unpopular stand — to face the financial oppressors and say, 'We won't allow your attempt to dominate the world to continue. We will oppose. We will stand up to you. And we will fight you.' *That* is what we have taking place in Germany in the years leading up to and during the Second World War. And when Germany said, 'We will not let you play the "we-are-the-victim" card,' the oppressors had another idea, a very good one as it turns out. They created the incredible fabrication known as the Holocaust."

As he was talking, Mr. R had been tapping keys and pictures had been flashing on and off the screen very quickly, some too quickly to recognize, I thought I saw a bank head office building and the desert — maybe Israel? I wasn't sure — and a couple of pictures of old Jewish men in those traditional clothes they wear. But the last picture was the one I would remember, even though I'd seen it before. It was the picture of all the naked bodies in the ditch. But this time, the picture zoomed in … once, twice, three times … until there was just one body. He left that picture on the screen and turned to face us.

"Jews died in the war, make no mistake about that. So did Catholics and Protestants, Germans, British, Americans, and Canadians. The war was a terrible thing. And if there was a holocaust that would have been a terrible thing too. And there is evidence that it did happen ... just as there is evidence that it did not. I ask only that you think about this question very carefully: Did the Holocaust happen? Do not let yourself be caught up in the agenda of a people who seeks compassion and pity and, when it is offered, conspire to use that outpouring of genuine human emotion by well-meaning people to further their goal of world domination."

Mr. R leaned toward us. "*Think*. Think and question and don't merely accept the popular version of history. But be forewarned. When you do that — when you have the courage and the integrity to oppose what is a popular, accepted position in our society, you will be criticized ... even ostracized. Who knows what that means?"

Ben had his hand up, but Mr. Retzlaff ignored him. "T-Ho, you remember what happened when you were up here at the front of the room and the rest of the class was piling on you pretty hard because of your fight with Marcia."

"I remember," T-Ho said and looked back at us. I thought he'd be laughing or at least smiling, but he looked pretty serious.

"You were ostracized, cast out of the group ... voted off the island (a few snickers). Not because you weren't good at some series of challenges that were put to you as part of a contest, but because you had done the unpopular thing. You had dared to take on a well-liked member of the class, one that happened to have a bunch of friends on her side."

121

Mr. R paced, much slower than usual, back and forth across the front of the classroom — always facing us as he walked, moving his eyes up and down the rows like he was looking at each one in turn.

"That is what can happen to you when you don't just accept what is said and written in the history books; when you question, when you challenge, and when you have the courage — and believe me, it requires courage — to say, 'I will decide for myself.'

"And when that happens ... when the criticism and the ostracism and the name calling and all the rest of it starts ..." The screen went blank behind Mr. R and the room was as dark as it had been at the start of the class. "When that happens, you have the one thing that makes *me* ... truly angry."

I'm not sure how much time passed as we sat there in the silent darkness, but I'd guess it was a minute. Except it was one of those deals when one minute feels like five.

The class ended and as we walked out of the room, Mr. Retzlaff still hadn't moved. Except he nodded his head just a little bit to let us know we could go.

We were out in the hall and walking to our next class and nobody was saying anything. We rounded the corner leading to the Common and saw kids crying and sitting at tables making cards and a poster with a picture of Mr. Saarkahn on it.

I'd totally forgotten that one of our teachers had died.

DECEMBER

One

When I finally got rid of my virginity it wasn't at all like getting it "smashed like a bug." And it wasn't with Patti. Or with Jen, The Six sex goddess.

See, another thing my brother told me is that a guy becomes a lot more popular with his ex once he has a new girlfriend. So maybe that's why Diana McNair phoned me on a Thursday and asked me to a party the next night at her friend's house.

And I went. I guess that decision falls into the "what was I thinking?" category.

I mean, I still thought Diana was mega-hot, no doubt about that. Sort of a cross between Avril Lavigne and Lindsay Lohan. Not a bad cross. Okay, maybe that's an exaggeration. But Diana *was* hot. She had like great hair — really dark and really curly. She was a little shorter than me, had an amazing smile that she didn't use nearly often enough, and there wasn't a whole lot wrong with her body. Actually, *nothing* was wrong with it.

I have to admit I still thought about her some-times, even though I really liked Patti. So the obvious question was why didn't I take Patti to the party. It's a question I've asked myself a couple of thousand times. Never have come up with an answer though.

I *did* ask myself why Diana had suddenly changed and didn't hate me anymore, but to be honest I didn't spend a lot of time on the subject. I guess I was just glad she'd phoned me.

Anyway, I went to the party.

Besides, it's not like Patti was my girlfriend or anything. We'd just gone out a few times. That's what I was saying to myself as I walked up the front steps of Diana's friend's house. I thought the friend's name was Elaine but I wasn't sure. I'd seen the house before but I'd never been inside.

Even in the light of the street lamp and the porch light, it was pretty easy to see this girl's family had money. Two-car garage, a pretty new BMW in the driveway, nice front yard with a couple of giant trees and a very cool winding sidewalk like you'd see leading up to a mansion. The place *wasn't* a mansion but it was quite a bit better than the Crockett residence.

"Alamo!" Diana answered the door and greeted me like I was the most important guest who would be attending that night. She kissed me on the cheek, took my jacket, and led me inside and straight to the drinks table.

I said hi to a few people on the way there and saw Hennie and Big Nose Kate sitting on the far side of the biggest living room I'd ever been in. The furniture looked like stuff BMW people would have and I glanced around, wondering if Elaine's parents would allow a party with booze in their house without being somewhere in the background to make sure nobody was puking on the hardwood.

Diana was still holding my arm and I was trying to figure out what exactly I'd done to get back in her good books. That thing my brother told me about the new girlfriend and the ex — I didn't remember that until later.

"You know Rain don't you?" she squeezed my arm.

"What?"

"Rain Masters? This is her house you're in, remember?"

I turned and Rain Masters was standing there smiling. I was real happy I hadn't called her Elaine. What kind of a name is Rain anyway? But hey, that guy in Coldplay, Chris something-or-other, the one that was married to Gwyneth Paltrow, isn't their kid named Apple?

"Hi … Rain," I smiled back at her.

"I have to borrow your girl for few minutes."

"Uh … sure."

They headed off in the direction of what I guessed was the kitchen.

Diana looked back over her shoulder. "I'll be back."

My girl. Right.

I pulled a beer out of a giant cooler full of ice and twisted the top off as I turned around to check out the room and the people in it. I started by looking up. It was like the place made you do that. The ceiling was really high with these wooden beams or whatever crisscrossing along the ceiling. A lot of glass.

As in very large windows and lots of them. The far wall of the place, the one that Hennie and Big Nose Kate were sitting and leaning against was just about all entertainment centre: a TV — I figured maybe a sixty-inch-screen — and a stereo system with a couple thousand components and speakers that were even bigger than the TV. As I looked around, I decided that the theme of the room was ... *big*. Yeah, the Masters family wasn't hurting.

The place had a smell to it too, kind of that new-carpet-shampoo smell. Except that there wasn't any carpet — just hardwood floor. Whatever was making that clean smell would have to be fairly powerful if this place was still going to smell like that in two or three hours.

"Hey." T-Ho had come to the table for a beer.

"Hey."

"Now how does someone as *un-jen-yoo-wine* as you get invited to a fancy-shmancy deal like this?"

To tell the truth, I'd kind of been wondering the same thing about him. I decided not to bring that up.

"Just lucky I guess."

T-Ho punched me on the arm ... pretty hard. "And what was all that interrogation crap you were giving me in the DQ the other night? About the Bidwell Plant and how I knew about it and a bunch of shit."

He leaned toward me, breathing beer on me as he said, "There's a lot of stuff I know. And if you ever get *jen-yoo-wine* maybe you'll get to know a few things too."

He walked off and disappeared into the crowd, which was okay with me. T-Ho can be a little hard to be around sometimes, and that situation doesn't improve as he takes on more beer.

I walked around the room taking the odd sip and doing the "hi, how ya doin'" thing with some kids I knew. There were lots I didn't.

I slid down onto the floor next to Hennie and Big Nose Kate. Hennie was telling a joke and I just caught the end. It sounded crude and Big Nose Kate and Hennie both laughed for a long time before they noticed I was there. Kate took a sip of something clear … probably vodka.

"Where is everybody? I saw T-Ho but where's the rest?"

Hennie shrugged. Big Nose Kate pointed. "Upstairs. There's a bunch of people up there. They're in the other kitchen, upstairs. I think Rain's parents are doling out some kind of snacks."

Two kitchens — that is shmancey. I nodded. At least the parent question had been answered. I reminded myself that if I had to puke I should take it outside.

Kate must have guessed what I was thinking. "They're cool. I've been to parties here before. They'll just go to bed after a while and let things roll."

"Nobody's ever wrecked the place?"

"Nobody's ever wrecked the place."

"What's with you and the lovely Diana?" Hennie grinned at me. "Looked to me like she thinks you're the man again."

"Yeah, I don't know. Maybe she thinks I won a lottery or something."

"I don't know about no lottery but it looks to me like you could score all right."

"Yeah, right. I don't think so. I'm pretty sure she still hates me … remember the dance? Maybe she just wants something."

Hennie's grin got bigger. "Yeah, she just might want somethin', mon." Hennie's Jamaican accent got more pronounced after a few drinks. He drew out every word in the sentence and then laughed his crazy laugh. Big Nose Kate smiled at me and nodded.

I downed the rest of the beer. "Think I'll get another. You guys okay?" I got to my feet.

"We're fine." Hennie pulled back the curtain that hung down from one of the giant windows. Behind it was a stash of beers, half a bottle of Smirnoff, and a plate of snacks that looked like it would feed a dozen people. I had to give Hennie credit; he was pretty good at gathering supplies.

Someone had cranked the music and nobody was talking much. No one was dancing either — it was mostly just sitting around, drinking, a little smoking weed (I wondered about the parents again) and heads moving to the music. A couple of people were making out — I didn't know them — and a couple of girls were all over each other not far from where Hennie and Big Nose Kate were sitting. They were watching the two girls.

I downed a couple of cheese crackers and was about halfway through my second beer when Diana came back. She grabbed my arm again and reached up and kissed me on the cheek. Then she put her lips against my ear and said, "I think you should come with me."

I set my beer down and she led me down a hall. We passed Rain and she smiled and said, "Have fun, you two."

Diana opened a door and pulled me into a room that led off the hall. I could see it was a bedroom in the few seconds before the door closed. Then it was pitch black in there and Diana didn't turn the light on. Her mouth was on mine and her tongue was doing some fairly magical things that I remembered from before. Except this time her hands were doing some things too — stuff that I *didn't* remember from before. She pulled me down on the bed and when I reached for her there wasn't the kind of almost-but-not-quite-giving-in that there'd been before. There was no *almost* at all. The only thing she said was in a breathless, panting sort of whisper. "You don't need to worry about a condom; I've got that handled."

Later I thought how stupid it was that I didn't question that little piece of information. Or give at least some thought to all the stuff that could have gone wrong — the stuff they tell you about at least once a month at school, pregnancy, HIV, some other STD … . But my main thought at that exact moment was, *thank god, because I've never carried a condom in my entire virgin-plagued life.*

It started and ended — way too fast. Diana was lying back on the bed and she was all, *ohmigod that was beautiful* and I was all, *what the hell happened?* Of course, I didn't say that out loud. I mean, it was good and it was cool and everything, but I had this voice inside my head — sort of, *okay, so I got laid, what now?*

I put my face up into Diana's neck, thinking *well, now that I've got that first one out of the way, let me show you what I can do.* But just like that she rolled onto her side and said, "I think you'd better go."

"What?"

"Alamo, I want you to go … now."

Jesus Christ.

It was a bit of a joke trying to get dressed in the dark, especially since my clothes were all wrapped up with Diana's. I was afraid I'd walk out of that bedroom with my T-shirt on inside out or, worse, with something of Diana's sticking out through a sleeve or something.

I was dressed and ready to go with my hand on the doorknob but I stopped. "Uh … Diana, I …"

"It was nice, Andy. It was. I just want you to go now."

"I'll … uh … see you at school?"

"Yeah."

I went out into the hall and back into the big living room. I grabbed a beer off the table, twisted off the top, and looked around. I was afraid every eye in the place would be on me and this would be like some huge April Fools' joke or something. But the only person who paid any attention to me at all was T-Ho. He got up from where he was sitting and walked over to me.

"Well, well, the look of a man satisfied — in fact, it looks like maybe you're finally getting a little more *jen-you-wine*, Alamo." He was grinning and nodding like he'd had a video camera on the whole thing. I actually glanced around to see if there were screens or anything, but I didn't see any.

I looked back at him, but decided the smartest thing right then would be to keep my mouth shut. No bragging. Actually I wasn't sure my performance in the bedroom deserved any bragging.

"And what about sweet Patti there, stud? What ... about ... the ... *girlfriend*?"

I hated the way he said it, but even more I hated the fact that when he said Patti's name it was the first time I'd thought of her since I'd got to the party. That was the second time in a week that something I should have been thinking about went right out of my head while I thought about something else.

I had a couple more swallows of beer and left.

Two

Hoax day in Mr. R's class. Actually it was the third and final hoax day. I was in the last group. There were only a few of us who hadn't done our presentations — Hennie and I from The Six, Gail Bannering, Ben the computer geek, and Patti.

Patti and I hadn't gone out since Rain Masters' party, but we'd hung out some at school and so far it didn't look like anybody had said anything to her. Diana had said hi to me in the hall a couple of times. The look on her face wasn't real friendly but it wasn't *I hope a Black Widow bites you on the ass* either.

To tell the truth I didn't know how to act with either of them. I didn't want to get back together with Diana or anything, which was good since it didn't look like that possibility even existed. I felt, I guess, nervous, whenever I saw her, mostly because I had no clue what I should say. And around Patti I felt bad, I really did. I'd cheated on her, sort of, and I wasn't proud of it. But more than anything I kept hoping that somehow she wouldn't find out.

Having to do the presentation in class helped to get my mind off women issues. I absolutely knew I was going to kick butt. I'd worked on my hoax for two days and two nights and I'd seen all the presentations so far and I was totally positive mine was better than all of them.

I even rehearsed my presentation in front of Mom and Dad. Actually that was kind of weird. My dad made a couple of suggestions that I thought were pretty good. After his second suggestion — about how to use my voice to convince people, Mom said, "Oh, that's a good idea, Larry. You're so much better at seeing things like that than I am. It must be your theatre background."

Theatre background? My dad? I knew he'd been in New York when he was in his early twenties but he'd never said anything about theatre. So, of course I asked.

He seemed almost embarrassed. "Yeah, I studied for a couple of years at a theatre school called Circle in the Square…. I guess I had a couple of small roles in some off-Broadway productions."

"You guess? That is *so* cool. My old man, the Broadway actor!"

"Off-Broadway."

I shook my head. "Still way cool."

Dad nodded and got up and went into the kitchen. Didn't want to talk about his acting career anymore.

"He sees it as a failure," Mom said after Dad was out of the room. "He went to New York convinced he'd set the acting world on fire. When he didn't, he came back home and has never done another thing with theatre. We very seldom even go to plays, except for the ones you guys do at school."

I'd had a part in a play called *Arsenic and Old Lace* back in middle school. I played a butler. I don't think I was very good.

But my dad had been an actor! In New York! It's strange how there's all this stuff about our parents we don't know. And I never would have found out about my dad the actor if it weren't for the hoax presentation.

It had taken only about five seconds to feel the excitement after I walked into Mr. R's classroom. The place was jumping … wall-to-wall energy. Like when it's the last day before Christmas break — that's how it felt. I was hoping I'd be first. I was ready.

But Mr. R called Gail Bannering first. She was Jake the tire guy's daughter. As Gail walked up there, I thought again about that night — Uncle Herm Night. Mostly I thought about what had happened afterward. The jokes in the hall had more or less gone away but there were still the smiles, some giggles from girls, behind-the-hand comments from the guys. It was like having a second nose. Nobody actually pointed to it. But I knew and they knew it was there.

I'd always liked Gail — she seemed nice enough — but I never thought she had much imagination. I was right. She did the Kennedy assassination — claimed the whole Lee Harvey Oswald thing was a hoax. Yeah, we've never heard *that* before. She probably rented that *JFK* movie, made a few notes, and bingo. Although

Mr. R did say we *could* use a hoax that was already out there. He seemed to like Gail's presentation.

Next was Ben. His was pretty good. It was a radio broadcast from sometime in the thirties by an actor named Orson Welles. I thought of my dad and how Orson Welles and Dad had both been actors. Anyway, this had been a radio play — kind of a takeoff on an H. G. Wells novel called *War of the Worlds*. Yeah, same as the Tom Cruise movie, I guess. But this was all done like a newscast that made it sound like it was really happening. Ben had some clips from the actual radio program and some amazing stats about all the panic it caused.

After Ben was finished, Jen put up her hand. "Does something count as a hoax if it wasn't meant to be a hoax? I read something about that radio broadcast, and they even had a thing at the start that told everybody it was a play. The reason all those people panicked is that they were dumber than shit."

I thought Jen would be in serious trouble for the "shit" comment, but Mr. R just shook his head. He was sort of smiling. "Bad word choice, Jen, and don't do it again. As for the hoax part, it may not have been intentional but it was probably the best career move Orson Welles ever made. My ruling is it counts."

Hennie was up next, talking about the "Paul McCartney's dead" hoax. I'd never heard of that one but when I saw the stuff the Beatles did on their album covers and in their songs I could see how they might have fooled some people. Hennie did a pretty good job.

Then it was my turn.

I'd checked out a bunch of the hoaxes that were already out there but I decided to make up my own. But now I was having serious second thoughts. Like my idea to sell a fake medical product was totally stupid and maybe not even a hoax at all. Anyway it was too late now. I'd have to go with it. I pulled on a green cap and shirt like you see doctors wearing in hospitals. I had a stethoscope around my neck.

I stepped to the front of the room and looked out at the class. I took a deep breath (my dad had given me that piece of advice) and started.

"My name's Dr. Dan," I said to a fair amount of snickering. That wasn't exactly what I was going for in terms of reaction, but I was hoping things might get better. The Dr. Dan thing, that was because I'd noticed that a lot of the guys (and women, too) on those radio and TV programs where they're selling some health product, had only one name, or at least they only *used* one name.

I smiled my best used-car salesman smile at the class and made sure I didn't look at Mr. R. I wasn't sure I'd get through the presentation if I saw his reaction, whatever it was. "The biggest concern people have these days is that they're going to die before they get everything done that they want to." I paced up and down in front of the class, using my voice like Dad had said to.

"Whether it's travelling to exotic places you've always wanted to see, watching your grandchildren grow up, or making one more million to add to the millions you've already made, you need more time ...

you need to live longer. Because let's face it — dying sucks. Especially when it happens before you're ready. That's why my dedicated team of assistants and I have created this amazing new product, Ten Plus, that comes with a money-back guarantee. Die before the guaranteed ten years and you get your money back."

Most of the class laughed at that part. I couldn't help myself and snuck a look over at Mr. R, but he was looking down writing notes on the pad in front of him. I couldn't tell if he was smiling.

"Six years in the laboratory and the result is a remarkable new formula that works very simply, really. It's all about the immune system. If your immune system is functioning as it should, you can fight off many of the diseases that take us out prematurely. Ten Plus acts as a stimulant to the immune system. Think of it like steroids for athletes. Except our product is legal, of course. Ten Plus enhances the performance of your body's defence system. Just take a package a day, mixed up in a tasty drink, and the results are instantaneous and amazing."

I held up three packages of Ten Plus. "To show you exactly what I mean, I'd like to call on three volunteers to sample Ten Plus and, before the end of this class, report what is happening with their bodies...."

I'd spent most of the night before thinking about who I should use for my test cases. I'd decided I wouldn't use any of The Six. I handed out the doses of my magic crap potion to Marcia Kiefer (perky and would try hard), Gail Bannering (cute, likable, and that no-imagination thing meant she wouldn't say something totally stupid just to get a laugh), and Ben the computer geek (would probably hit me up to let him design the product website. He'd *want* it to work.).

The stuff looked harmless, kind of like cola, only thicker. Each sample was about a third of a glass. I would have liked to give them more but I was afraid they might take too long drinking it and kill my presentation. All three looked at it suspiciously at first, which is why I had a fourth batch ready. I drank it down, and wiped my lips with the back of my sleeve. "Satisfyingly delicious," I said.

Marcia looked over at Mr. R, who looked at me, all serious. "I don't think anyone in this class would encourage a classmate to drink anything that wasn't appropriate, am I right about that, Mr. Crockett, uh … Dr. Dan?"

"Yes sir," I said, "there isn't anything in Ten Plus that will cause any problems for anyone … and heck, that extra ten years thing is a pretty good deal." I grinned and most of the people in the class laughed.

All three of my test pilots drank the stuff — Ben and Marcia in one gulp, Gail kind of sipping hers.

"That concludes my demonstration, class, except for the testimony of these three individuals, your classmates, who will report back to us in fifteen minutes with what I predict will be quite amazing findings. Thank you."

The class applauded, including Mr. R. I wasn't sure but I thought I'd seen him give a little nod in my direction. Of course I had no idea what my three guinea pigs were going to say. But I figured if the stuff tasted okay and didn't actually make any of them feel *bad*, I just might get some decent reports. I mean, all there was in Ten Plus was Blast Off, which was the latest (and strongest) cola-flavoured energy drink, a couple of dissolved baby Aspirins, and some squares of melted milk chocolate. I knew it tasted good and I was counting on having that little shot of energy maybe get me at least one "Holy crap, Dr. Dan, the stuff really works." And if it didn't, so what — it was supposed to be a hoax, wasn't it?

But what happened in the next fifteen minutes of the class kind of blew Ten Plus right out of the water, In fact, nobody, not even Mr. R, bothered to ask Marcia or Ben or Gail how they were feeling after the next presentation … the one that Patti Bailer gave.

Three

I thought Patti looked especially hot that day. Without trying. She was wearing this burnt orange up-to-the-neck sweater that did a better job of getting me excited about her ... uh ... upper torso ... than the all-cleavage tops that some of the girls wore some of the time. And Jen wore *all* the time.

Not a lot of makeup. And Patti's jeans were just the right tightness. Thing is, Patti was someone you could take home to the parents, but the guys at school would totally notice at the same time.

As I watched her move things around at the front of the room to get ready for her presentation I kept thinking how glad I was that no one had ratted to her about Diana and me. Every day that went by I figured I was a little safer. And every day that went by convinced me more and more that Patti was the one I wanted to be with and that the night with Diana had been totally stupid.

I knew that wasn't what I was supposed to be thinking about at that exact moment but I couldn't help it. This was the girl I was going out with and *she looked hot.*

Patti set her laptop on a front row desk, clicked it on, and turned to face us. She didn't take a deep breath. She looked nervous but not terrified. One thing I'd learned about Patti Bailer: She was a confident person. She'd been shy at first but it wasn't a scared-shy. Patti just didn't talk if she didn't have something to say. Like during those first few phone calls. I liked that about her. Actually, she could have run classes on talking (and not talking) for The Six. Especially Hennie and Jen. I figured their mouths started working at about the same time their eyes opened every morning.

Maybe it was partly because my own presentation was out of the way or maybe it was because it was this particular girl who was about to present, but I had a feeling this was going to be a very cool few minutes.

"We've heard about pictures in this class," she started, "and we've been told they can be used to convey misinformation — and they can. For example … "

Patti moved her mouse and clicked it twice. On the screen was the picture Mr. R showed us of him standing in front of the bus, looking like he was about to be hit. Patti clicked again and this time the same picture appeared, except there was a cute little dog standing next to Mr. R. Now it looked like both of them were about to be shmucked by the bus.

Click. Whoa. The third photo in the sequence very clearly showed Mr. R kicking the dog into the path

143

of the bus while standing safely out of the way himself. After a few seconds of surprised silence everybody laughed at pretty well the same time and the whole class gave Patti a nice round of applause. It had been a pretty cool trick and it was funny. I glanced over at Mr. R. He was smiling, but he wasn't applauding. And he didn't look like he was having quite as much fun as the rest of us.

Up at the front, Patti defintely *wasn't* smiling. Actually, she looked school teacher-ish. "Now we all know that Mr. Retzlaff was making a point — he wasn't really trying to convince us that he'd been run over by a bus, any more than I was trying to prove that he actually kicked a dog in front of that same bus. The wonders of Photoshop, right, Mr. Retzlaff?"

A lot of us looked over at Mr. R. He gave a little smile and nod in Patti's direction.

Patti smiled back at him then looked at the class. "Mr. Retzlaff (I noticed she never called him Mr. R) has told us that there have been times in our history when a certain group of people have furthered their own agenda by using misinformation — by convincing the rest of the world, through words or pictures or both — that they have been persecuted and victimized in order to pursue their goal of world domination. I agree that would be bad. In fact, if *any* group of people or even an individual, say a leader of some group, takes advantage of other people's trust to mislead or misrepresent — to present something as truth that really isn't — that *to me* is one of the greatest abuses of a position of authority and trust that can happen. But it actually, unfortunately, happens a lot. So let's look at some famous examples of people who have done that …"

Patti returned to her computer and spoke over her shoulder as she tapped keys. A picture of a young guy — maybe thirty-something, pretty good looking, former high school basketball-star look to him. Patti hit another key and the picture changed. This one was of a fire — this huge walled-in area of some kind with buildings in behind and smoke pouring out of just about the whole place.

"Waco, Texas, 1993. A man named David Koresh. He was the leader of a cult group called the Branch Davidians that walled themselves into their compound and held off the authorities for several weeks. The stand-off ended with many of Koresh's followers dying in this fire when the authorities went in to get them."

Another *click*. Older guy in a sweater and ball cap that had UCLA printed on it. The picture changed. This was of an abandoned place, you couldn't really tell where. No, not abandoned. Patti changed the image and zeroed in on one area — where a couple of guys and were manoeuvring what looked like a body bag. Next to the bag there seemed to be two more bodies. One looked like a kid — a little black kid.

"Jonestown, Guyana, 1978. James Jones convinced his followers to commit mass suicide by taking poison, but reports afterward said that some people were shot. It was thought that those who wouldn't take the poison were shot by James Jones' guards. These people died, just like the ones in Waco, Texas, because they were willing to believe totally and unquestioningly in the teachings of a trusted leader."

Patti changed the picture. This one was hard to make out. It was a truck with something on the back, although it was pretty hard to tell what. "And then there's that rather famous modern-day hoax — the one that led to a war in Iraq that took thousands of lives and is still taking them today; a war that was started because the American president and the British prime minister were able to convince their countrys' citizens that Iraq was in possession of weapons of mass destruction. It wasn't, but that little fact didn't stop all this …"

Patti clicked the computer keys a few times in rapid succession and horrible pictures came on the screen in a sort of collage. The pictures were changing so fast I couldn't really keep up with what I was seeing. But it didn't really matter. They were pictures all of us had seen on TV and in the newspapers. Blood-spattered bodies, burning cars, markets, restaurants, shops — all blown apart. Some of the pictures showed horribly dead and dying people, some of them soldiers or police, although it was hard to tell which.

I noticed something just then. Patti had had some music playing during her slide show, very softly up until now. The music had been getting louder for the last couple of minutes but now, suddenly, it stopped. On the screen was one picture — a little kid with blood all over his face. It was one of those black-and-white shots — like the ones Mr. R had shown before. Same time period, same part of the world — that's what it looked like. I guessed he was a Jewish kid, but I wasn't sure. Somehow this one image had a greater impact than all the ones of peoples' bodies piled in ditches. I don't know why that was.

Then the picture changed again and we were back to an ordinary looking guy — suit, tie, glasses, tan, nice smile. Patti had been looking at the screen, but now she turned to look at us again.

And suddenly Mr. R was at the front of the classroom, standing next to Patti and closing the lid on her laptop. "I'm afraid we're getting into some political areas that really don't qualify as hoaxes. This is all very interesting but we'll have to bring this to a conclusion. Thank you, Patti." Mr. R's voice sounded different — flat, harder, kind of like parents sound when they're making the "I just found your weed stash" announcement. The only other time I'd ever heard him sound like that was when I'd lost in the wrestling regionals.

"I have one more sequence to show the class." Patti didn't look like she was about to give in easily.

"I'm sure you do, but we'll have to wrap it up now for the reason I just stated. And as I said at the outset, there is a time limit and you've exceeded that limit. So thank you, Patti. How about a nice hand for all of our presenters today."

Patti hadn't moved. There was a small amount of applause.

Mr. R was nodding. "I'm going to let you guys go a few minutes early today. Unit exam next day — open notebook. Then it's on to the Cold War. Thanks everyone," He smiled the big smile at us.

There were a few things about that day I didn't get, at least not right away. When I asked Patti after class who the guy in the last picture was, she wouldn't tell me. And the thing about the time limit. When Mr. R went up to stop Patti's presentation, I looked down at my watch because I wanted to make sure I'd still have time to check in with my three Ten Plus testers. She was under the five-minute limit for sure.

And what was the deal with dismissing the class early? It kind of killed my big finale. I guess it didn't matter though. When we got our marks after all the presentations were done, I got an A.

So did Patti.

Four

I had a lot on my mind, which is probably why that first time I saw the old lady they called Numbers didn't seem like any big deal. I was with The Six — we were in town and I was leaning against the Biscayne listening to Hennie tell this joke about some guy trying to join the Mile High Club in a single-seater airplane.

He barely got the punch line out when T-Ho was suddenly standing tall and looking serious. "There she is."

The laughing stopped and we all looked around.

Jen said, "There *who* is?"

Which I thought was a good question. I didn't see anybody but an old woman shuffling across the street with a couple of grocery bags in her arms. I didn't figure she was anybody who would get T-Ho all mega-focused.

I was wrong. "Numbers is what they call her." He didn't take his eyes off the woman as he spoke. "She's nasty and there's a lot of people who think somebody should do something about her."

I looked again at the old lady. *Nasty?* Mostly she looked like she'd have barely made it over the curb when she finally got across the street.

I looked at T-Ho to see if he was putting us on. He wasn't. His eyes still hadn't left the woman as she navigated the street, looking like she was going to drop the grocery bags any second. I figured that, since T-Ho had lived in Parkerville forever, he must have seen the old lady before. I wondered if he always got this intense whenever she was around. Because right at that moment, T-Ho was *real* intense. No, that's not right. Intense isn't enough. The look on T-Ho's face as he stared at the woman was pure anger … maybe even hate. I noticed Rebel was also paying big-time attention to the old lady, though he didn't seem to be as pissed off as T-Ho.

And that was it. Eventually the woman disappeared into the drug store on the other side of the street and Hennie — I think he was mad that his joke got sort of cut off — launched into another one.

I kind of forgot the incident not long after that, mostly because I didn't know who Numbers was and I wasn't really interested in some old lady who didn't amount to a whole lot in my life, even if she was "nasty."

And like I said, I had some things on my mind. That was about the time things were getting sort of interesting between Patti and me — interesting and crappy. She knew about Diana and me — actually she'd known about it almost right after it happened. But she hadn't said anything. We even went out a couple of times.

I noticed she seemed kind of serious but I thought that was just Patti being Patti; she was usually pretty serious.

She hadn't seemed mad or anything, although I noticed the physical stuff had pretty much cooled off. Then one night — as I was trying to get my head around a physics problem that reminded me how much better the world would be if nobody had ever invented physics — the phone rang. It was Patti.

"I was hoping maybe you could meet me in the park," was what she said.

It was cold outside, maybe a couple of degrees above zero, but even if it had been minus thirty, I'd have slammed my physics book shut and been out the door before Patti could hang up the phone. Which is about the way it happened.

I got to the park first — it was about a block from the school — and walked around until Patti got there. For some reason, I was really nervous — first-date nervous.

"Hi," I said.

"Hi."

Then nothing. It was like those first few phone calls. *And this time I hadn't written down any conversation topics.*

Even though it was cold we sat on a park bench, both of us shivering. I tried to pretend I wasn't that cold but I don't really think it was working. My teeth were chattering and I kept stamping my feet on the ground to keep them from turning to blocks of ice.

I wasn't sure why Patti had wanted to have a

conversation that could result in major freaking frost-bite, but she leaned forward and kissed me lightly on the mouth and right away I didn't give a damn about the cold.

"It was my fault you didn't get to finish your hoax presentation," she told me. "Retzlaff wanted to end mine and he couldn't do that without losing the end of yours too. I'm totally sorry."

"No worries," I grinned at her. "We both got an A so it doesn't really matter."

"Actually it does," Patti shook her head. "It matters a lot."

I wasn't sure why but I didn't want her to think I was like major dull, so I just nodded my head. "I still don't get what happened — why Mr. R cut you off that day."

This time she told me. "The guy in that last picture?"

"Yeah?"

"He's a Holocaust denier. Famous for it, actually. He's a doctor and was even elected to office in Saskatchewan. Twice. Wrote a couple of books about how the Holocaust didn't really happen — how it's all a big conspiracy ... yeah, pretty famous guy."

"And you think Mr. R shut you down because you put that guy's picture up there?"

Patti shook her head. "No, he shut me down because he was afraid of what I was going to say about the guy."

I couldn't see that. I couldn't see Mr. R being afraid of something like that. But I nodded again.

Then we talked about Mr. Saarkahn — Patti had

gone to the funeral a couple of days before. "There were a lot of people — a lot of kids from school."

I was still thinking about whether I should be explaining why I hadn't gone to the funeral when she said, "I guess we won't be going out anymore, Andy."

The way she said it, it sounded like maybe her parents didn't like me or something. But, of course, that wasn't it.

"I wanted to see if I'd be okay with what you did, but I guess I'm not."

"What did I do?" A stupid thing to say, I know, but she kind of caught me by surprise and I guess I was hoping that by some miracle she was talking about something else. Something like I'd forgotten to phone her when I said I would or I'd accidentally insulted her sister — one of those things you can apologize all over the place for and maybe she gets over it. But it wasn't any of those things.

"Diana told me about it the day after the party." Patti's face got kind of puckered and scrinchy, but I could see she didn't want to cry. "You don't have to say anything. In fact, I'd rather that you didn't. I thought maybe I could deal with it. But I can't get it out of my head."

She handed me my math book, which would have been hilarious if it wasn't part of me losing Patti. Most guys get their ring back or some very cool item that meant a lot to both people. All Patti had of mine was my math textbook. And now as she was ending it with me she remembered to give it back. Totally thorough and thoughtful right to the end.

Then she got up and walked off. And I realized that

I'd said exactly four words — *what did I do* — as my girlfriend was breaking up with me.

Girlfriend. Ex-girlfriend.

Damn.

As I thought about it later — that's *all* I thought about — I figured it out. Diana McNair, who *had* still hated my guts, definitely got the last laugh. The ultimate revenge. But what girl does that? What girl goes to bed with you so she can wreck your relationship with somebody else? Okay, maybe in movies.

I thought back on what had been going on since the party. Nothing, that's what. I'd stop in the hall to talk to Diana and she'd smile at me and keep going. No fake gagging, no giving me the finger — just the smile, then she'd walk on. Except it wasn't a real nice smile, you know what I mean? It wasn't a *you're very cool, Alamo* smile or even a *I'm kind of shy after what we did together* smile. I guess it was more of a *gotcha* smile — like Mr. R in the picture after he had us thinking he'd been hit by the bus.

Of course I didn't recognize the smile then. I just thought *fine, she doesn't want to talk but she's okay with me*. Which was pretty well perfect. I mean, I didn't want to get back together with Diana — mostly I just wanted that whole night to go away and let me carry on with Patti. And I guess I was wishing so hard for that to happen that I thought it *was* happening. Wrong. Dead wrong.

Yeah, things on my mind. I really *liked* Patti — I don't know about love. I wasn't sure I'd even know how to tell if that was what it was. But I hated that she wasn't my girlfriend anymore. I really hated that.

There was more. I had just found out the Biscayne needed a new radiator *and* water pump — at the same time. Yeah, *that* doesn't suck.

And that's also about the time this guy named Garth Redlake came around and started asking questions about Mr. R. The first time was at Joey's Pizza. Joey had just brought me a six-inch version of "Twist and Shout" — all the pizzas at Joey's are named after Beatles songs. Since Patti was out of my life forever, I was twisting and shouting by myself. So I didn't mind when a tall guy who didn't look much older than my brother — maybe not even as old — slid into the booth across from me and said, "You're Andy Crockett, right, *Alamo* Crockett?"

I swallowed way faster than I wanted to because the bite I was working on was like killer hot, and nodded. The guy stuck out his hand and said, "Garth Redlake, *Centennial Times*."

I wiped off my hand and shook his and looked down at my pizza. Joey came by the table. "You want something?" he asked my uninvited guest.

"Just a Coke."

Joey walked off and Garth looked at me then at my pizza then at me again. "Go ahead and eat, I don't want to interrupt your dinner — what is that, a 'Paperback Writer'?"

"'Twist and Shout.' It's pepperoni, mushrooms, and green peppers … pretty good."

Garth nodded. "Looks good. I mean it, go ahead. I was just wondering if I could … I'm writing this story for the paper on some of the teachers who've been around for a long time. I was hoping I could ask you about Mr. Retzlaff."

"I've seen you around here before, haven't I?"

"Yeah, the paper's sent me to cover a couple of stories down here. I cover most of Parkerville's sports. Including wrestling."

I nodded and took a swallow of pop. "I thought you looked familiar. That's where I must've seen you."

"And I was here a couple of years back — wrote a story on the school."

Maybe I should have thought more about that, maybe asked him about it, but I didn't.

"So, it's okay then?" he asked again. "If I ask you some stuff?"

He didn't seem like I thought reporters should be — all aggressive, like cops but with notebooks. Actually Garth Redlake didn't have a notebook, at least he didn't have one in front of him.

"Mr. R? Sure, go ahead."

Joey brought Garth's Coke and he took a long drink before he spoke again. "I've heard he's a pretty amazing teacher. What do you think of him?"

I nodded. "Pretty amazing's about how I'd put it. I've had some okay teachers before — and some crappy ones — but Mr. R … uh, Mr. Retzlaff, he's the best, no contest."

"What makes him so special, do you think?"

I took a bite of pizza, worked on it for a while

before I answered. "Well, he's a cool guy. I think every kid at Parkerville thinks that, but that's not the main thing. It's what he does to make his classes like mega-interesting. It's like you can't wait for the next day so you can get back to Mr. R's class."

"You said he was cool. What's cool about him?"

I thought back to the dance but I didn't figure Garth Redlake would get it. It was one of those you-had-to-be-there moments. I sipped my drink. "He knows every kid in the school. And he cares about every one of them … us."

"Would you say he makes you think?"

"For sure. That's one of the best things about Mr. R. He makes you think *and* he gets you looking at stuff in a different way than a lot of teachers or even the textbooks do. Usually, school is all 'this is the way it is and don't think about it, just remember it' … but that's not how Mr. R does it."

That's when Garth dug out his notebook. It looked like it had been his notebook since before television was invented. I thought he'd have one of those little tape recorders, but all he had was the beat-up notebook and two pencils, both of them looked like they had recently been sharpened. He'd taken them from the inside pocket of a blazer that was all checks and squares. It looked older than the notebook except it wasn't tattered; it actually looked kind of okay.

"Is my name going to be in the paper?"

Garth looked at me and shook his head. "Only if you want it to be. I'm talking to lots of kids and people in the community as well. Some have said they don't want their names mentioned. So it's like, 'one Parkerville student said, *you can't wait for the next day so you can get back to Mr. R's class.*'"

I thought about that.

"Of course, if you'd rather have your name associated with the quote, I can do that."

I took a mouthful of pizza and shook my head. When I'd swallowed, I said, "I'm fine with having my name left out of it."

"No worries." Garth scribbled something in his notebook that I couldn't read — it was upside down and messy.

"Which social class do you have Mr. Retzlaff for?"

"Social 10."

"That's Twentieth-Century World History, isn't it?"

"Uh-huh." I liked the short answer questions because they allowed to me to get through more pizza. At first I'd been kind of uncomfortable eating in front of a stranger, but I was also hungry so now I was eating every chance I got.

"So that's the two world wars and Hitler and the Holocaust, right?"

"Only the Second World War. We took the first last year."

"I heard he has some interesting views about the Holocaust and Jews in general."

It was a statement, not a question, so I wasn't sure if I was supposed to say anything. But I also thought he was maybe saying something negative about Mr. R.

"Mr. R has interesting views about pretty well everything. That's one of the things that makes him so excellent. Plus, he wants us to think for ourselves — you know, question stuff."

"So what happens when you question *him*?"

I shrugged. "I think he's okay with it."

Which wasn't totally true. The only person who'd ever really had an issue with Mr. R was Patti and thinking back on it, I didn't think Mr. R *was* okay with it. There was that thing with her presentation and cutting her off. Of course, that might have been because of how Patti went about it … sort of wanting to get in his face. Anyway, I didn't say anymore to Garth on that topic.

"So do you think your view of Jews is different now than it was before you started the class?"

"I didn't have a view. I doubt if I'd ever thought about Jews or the Holocaust or any of that stuff before. That's another good thing about Mr. R. I'm thinking about them now. All of us are. Somebody else could be teaching the same course and it would be a total yawner. This isn't."

Garth finished his drink and looked like he was trying to decide whether to leave or not. He hadn't written anything else in his notebook so I figured I hadn't been much help with his story.

"Would you say Mr. R is your favourite teacher this year?"

I shook my head. "Mr. R is my favourite teacher of all time."

"What would you do if you found out a teacher was telling you things that weren't totally accurate …

maybe teaching stuff he believes rather than the way things actually are?"

"You talking about Mr. R?"

"Any teacher … say it *was* Mr. Retzlaff."

"That isn't the way it is." I set the slice of pizza I'd been working on down on my plate. "That isn't how it is at all. Like I said, he wants us to think, not to take something as real or true just because we read it in a textbook or saw it on TV or something."

"Would you say Mr. R is anti-semitic?"

"Which is?"

"Against Jewish people. Anti-Semites hate Jews."

That was a tough one. I thought about it for quite a while. "I'd say no. Not hate. He doesn't like what the Jews are trying to do — like trying to take over the world and how they exaggerate a lot of the stuff about the Holocaust and all that. I'd say that really pisses off Mr. R, but I never heard him say he hates them or anything."

"But he did say the Holocaust didn't happen?"

"No, not that it didn't happen — just that it wasn't like the stuff we read in the history books and stuff like that."

"And that the Jews are to blame for what has happened to them throughout history?"

That was another one I really had to think about. Answering all these questions was hard … kind of confusing. I tried to remember exactly what Mr. R had said — I remembered the "playing the sympathy card" thing he'd talked about, but I couldn't recall for sure what he'd said about the Jews throughout history.

"I'm not sure. I don't think he said that exactly."

"What about the word hoax? Did he say that in referring to the Holocaust?"

So Garth knew about the hoax discussion. That meant he must have talked to some other kids in the class.

"Well, we did some cool stuff about hoaxes — and I guess it was all to do with the Holocaust. In a way, I guess." I said "I guess" twice mostly because I wasn't happy with my answer. I didn't want Mr. R to look bad and I wasn't sure that what I was saying would make him look good.

"Mr. R is an excellent teacher — the best I've ever had." I knew I'd already told him that but I wanted it out there again.

Garth nodded and wrote in his notebook.

"Sure, Andy ... Alamo." He looked up at me. "One last thing. On the Holocaust: Would you say you share the view that it was exaggerated — a hoax — part of the Jewish plan for world domination?"

I was wishing this would end. "Like I said, I'm going to try harder to not just accept things I read or hear. I'm going to try to decide for myself about things that happened or didn't happen. And stuff that's going on in the world now, too. And that's because of Mr. R."

I liked that last answer — felt a lot better about what I'd said that time.

Garth stood up. "I appreciate your time. And I'll make sure anything I use from you will be anonymous as you requested. Hope I didn't cause you to have to eat cold pizza." He smiled at me.

"I like cold pizza." I could have added that it didn't burn your mouth when you were trying to eat while reporters are interviewing you. But I didn't. Instead I took a bite as Garth Redlake turned and walked out of Joey's.

Five

I think it was about a week later that I was sitting in the Dairy Queen doing some homework when Lou and Jen came in and sat in the booth across from me. They might have sat with me if I hadn't had my books and stuff all over the table.

It didn't matter because we kind of visited across the aisle. For a couple of minutes, we just talked about the usual stuff — movies, music, school. Jen even asked me if I'd made up with Patti. I just shook my head. Then, just out of the blue, the conversation completely shifted. They were both, like, "Numbers is this creepy old woman and she's bad for the town" — the same stuff that T-Ho had said. I can't remember it all but there was quite a bit more. About all I got out of it was that Numbers was somebody that nobody liked and nobody should.

There was one thing that seemed like a pretty big deal to both of them. The old lady lived really close to the Snow White Dairy.

"Have you ever walked by her in the street?" Jen waved her hand in front of her face.

When I shook my head, she added, "The woman stinks."

"Like cowshit, man."

I was having a little trouble with that. First of all, The Six wasn't always a shining example of great personal hygiene. And secondly, I doubted that living near something that smelled bad meant that *you* smelled bad. Although there was one summer we had a family of skunks that lived under our house until Dad could get rid of them. I think we all smelled a little skunky for a while. Didn't have the neighbours dropping over much that summer. Still, if somebody smells bad it doesn't really make them — what was it? — nasty.

T-Ho and Rebel talked to me about Numbers a few more times after that. Mostly they were on about how she gave the town a bad image, how she stunk like cowshit all the time, how she lived in an eyesore of a house that everybody hated, and how she was just all-around bad.

I didn't get why there was this sudden big interest in some old lady who (maybe) smelled bad and lived in a crappy house. Ever since we'd seen her downtown that time, it seemed like she was The Six's favourite topic of conversation. I sort of tried to find out why, but at first T-Ho wouldn't say anything more than, "You wouldn't get it. You need to be *jen-yoo-wine* to understand."

That told me exactly nothing. So I didn't pay a lot of attention. Except I asked a few people why the woman was called Numbers. Nobody seemed to know. I heard a few theories: Jen, who is all about nicknames, said it had to do with how many husbands she'd had. That sounded like a Jen theory, all right; Lou told me he'd heard that the old lady was a former girlfriend of a Mafia boss and she'd been in charge of the *numbers racket* (I didn't know what the "numbers racket" was and neither did Lou); and my dad, who had made a point of learning a lot about the town and its people, just shrugged when I asked him.

"I know the lady you're talking about, though I don't know her well," he told me. "And I've heard her called that but I don't know why — what it means."

I didn't think about Numbers anymore after that. Until December 23. Two days before Christmas, and the last day of school before the break.

"Alamo."

I was trying to find my copy of *To Kill a Mockingbird* in the piles of stuff that made my locker look like a tsunami site. I turned around and T-Ho was standing there. T-Ho had come looking for me exactly once in my life. That was one night not long after I started at Parkerville. The Crap Wagon was toast and The Six needed a car — my dad's car — to go into the city for something, I can't remember what it was.

So I guessed he probably needed wheels again, except this time it would be the Biscayne. I was wrong.

"Hey, man, why don't you stop by the Dairy Queen after school. We need to chat."

I didn't get a chance to answer or even think about it because he walked off down the hall without waiting even half a second. I figured T-Ho wasn't used to having people say, "I don't think so" when he suggested something.

Twenty minutes after school ended I drove the Biscayne into the parking lot of the DQ. The Crap Wagon was already there so I knew it wasn't my car T-Ho wanted. I grabbed a chocolate-chip-cookie-dough Blizzard and slid into the booth next to Rebel and across from T-Ho. That was different too, the two of them being without the rest of The Six. That had been happening more and more lately: T-Ho and Rebel had become the two guys who kind of hung out even without the others.

They both nodded and worked their shakes without saying anything right away.

T-ho belched and looked across the table at me. "So, the thing of it is, Alamo, as you know, you have had a lot of trouble getting to be *jen-yoo-wine*, right?"

What I wanted to say was, *what the fuck does that even mean?*

What I said was, "Yeah, I guess so."

"Yeah, I guess so," T-Ho repeated and nodded. I noticed Rebel was nodding too. I guess they were trying to be dramatic, but actually they reminded me of a couple of bobble-head dolls. And I noticed something else, too. In the time between the end of school and now, both of them had drank enough to smell like booze. I didn't think they were actually drunk but I could definitely smell alcohol on them.

"But now that's all gonna change." T-Ho was near the bottom of his shake and his straw made that scratchy slurping sound. "We have decided to give the town a Christmas present."

"A Christmas present."

"Uh-huh."

"Uh-huh." It was the first sound Rebel had made.

"And we're going to let you be a part of it."

"Be a part of what?"

"Here's the deal, Alamo … we are going to do something about this Numbers bitch. When I say we are going to do something about her, I mean we are going to burn down that piece-of-shit house she lives in."

What are you supposed to say when your sort of friend announces he's going to burn down someone's house? I guess your first reaction is you don't believe it.

I didn't believe it. "You're kidding, right?"

"Not kidding. Not kidding at all."

"Are you totally crazy? In the first place, people go to jail for burning down other people's houses. In the second place, why? What's the big deal with some old lady who lives by a smelly dairy? Who gives a shit?"

"Well, see, there you go again, Alamo, not getting it. One of the reasons you ain't *jen-yoo-wine* is that you just don't get it. It turns out that a lot of people give a shit. Take me, for instance. I give a shit. And Rebel here, he gives a shit too."

Rebel nodded.

"'Cause you see, Alamo, we are both *jen-yoo-wine*, which is something you don't understand and which is why there are only six people in The Six."

I didn't have an answer for any of that because none of it made any sense. I didn't say anything.

"And somebody else who gives a shit — Mr. R, that's who, A-la-mo."

"Let me get this straight. Are you telling me that Mr. R wants to see some old lady's house burned down?"

"Not just any old lady, A-la-mo. An old *Jew* lady."

I shook my head. It still didn't make even a little bit of sense.

"Let me explain it to you." T-Ho leaned forward and stared hard at me. "The Bidwell Plant."

"What?"

"The Bidwell Plant, for Chrissake. Are you deaf?"

"I heard you, I just don't get —"

"That old Jew lady burned it down. Burned it down because she hated her job. Hated her boss. So she used explosives, burned the place down, and then came back into the plant during the fire and supposedly saved some guy's ass … a guy that wouldn't have needed any help if the Jew bitch hadn't blown the place up and set fire to it in the first place."

"Okay, but what does any of that have to do with Mr. R?"

T-Ho leaned back, looked around, and took a couple of pulls on his milk shake. Got nothing but air. Then he leaned forward again.

"Have you heard anything the man has said all year? He hates that stuff — he hates that this … woman starts a fire, all but kills some poor shmuck of a janitor's assistant, who gets his leg broke in the explosion so he can't get out, and she supposedly drags him out and saves his life. She was like this big celebrity after the fire for saving this guy and all the time she was the one who caused it. And Mr. R said the guy had pretty well dragged his own ass out of there and she just came along at the end to look like a hero."

I swallowed a spoonful of Blizzard and looked at Rebel and T-Ho. It was like they had suddenly become Mr. R's two favourite students. That was another part of this I didn't totally get. I wondered when they first heard about the Bidwell Plant. I was betting it was a few days before the time we all stopped at the ruins.

"Mr. R has hated what she did — Numbers — he's hated her pretty well all his life. But, of course, he can't do anything about it."

"Why? I don't get that. Why can't Mr. R do something about her if she's that bad?"

T-Ho looked at Rebel. "See what I mean?" Rebel nodded.

T-ho leaned forward in the booth and stared hard at me. "Because he's Mr. R, genius. He's a good guy. And good guys can't be getting after old ladies even if they're bad bitches."

"But in class he said —"

"I need you to listen to me. Mr. R can't do this."

Rebel snapped his fingers. "But we can."

"And here's the cool part, A-la-mo. We are going to let you in on the deal. You get to be *jen-you-wine* for the first time in your life. You come with us, we burn the old lady's place down, and everybody's happy. Mr. R is happy, everybody in town is happy, and Rebel and me, we're happy too."

It was all starting to make sense. The time I'd seen Mr. R with T-Ho and Rebel after school — all buddied up. And the time Mr. R talked to me, told me — what had he said? — "We all can count on you when the time is right. It's important that you don't miss *this* opportunity." So this was the opportunity? Burning down the old lady's house …

I looked at T-Ho then at Rebel then back at T-Ho. "Did Mr. R say that's what he wanted — to burn the house down?"

"Hell no, he didn't say those words. But sometimes you just know what the right thing is without it being spelled out. The woman is a *Jew*."

For a second I wondered if T-Ho had ever spoken that word before this year's social class. But did that matter? It seemed like the whole town hated the woman. And Mr. R hated her. So, what if they were right … T-Ho and Mr. R? What if this *was* the opportunity? My opportunity …

"When are you —"

"And to show you just how happy me and Rebel are gonna be, The Six is done, there's no more Six after this. It's The Seven and you, A-la-mo, become totally *jen-yoo-wine*."

Genuine.

"When?" I asked a second time.

"Tomorrow night."

"It's Christmas freaking Eve!"

"Remember what I said about presents? What better time to give the people of Parkerville a present?"

"Does Mr. R know about this? That it's tomorrow night?"

T-Ho put a finger against his lips. "Shh, Alamo. Shh. Nobody knows anything, right, Rebel man?"

Rebel grinned. "Nobody knows anything."

"Shit."

"Yeah. So are you in, A-la-mo? Are you in and *jen-yoo-wine* or are you gonna sit there and say 'shit' and just be A-la-mo, the guy who was almost one of The Seven? Make up your mind because we don't have a lot of time."

All I wanted was to think, not to have T-Ho and Rebel sitting there watching me and talking to me. I just wanted to think. But there wasn't time for that.

I wanted to go with them. And I didn't want to go. I thought back to the time I'd seen the old lady crossing the street with her grocery bags. *Maybe I should go along just to make sure T-Ho and Rebel don't do something really stupid. Yeah, nice try. Okay, Alamo, this is your chance to do something that matters. That people might actually notice. That* Mr. R *might notice.*

"Yeah, I'm in."

"Well, god-*damn*." T-Ho grinned at me. "Remember the Alamo!" We knocked knuckles and the two of them stood up. "Tomorrow night. We meet by the dairy. Bring your car ... just in case." And they were gone.

Just in case what? I couldn't ask because the Crap Wagon was already rumbling out of the DQ parking lot.

But at least now I had time to think. And the more I thought about the plan the more I liked it. An old

171

Jew woman who Mr. R hated. Okay, maybe he didn't hate her, but he hated what she'd done, right? She'd started a fire and now we'd start one. What did they call that? Full circle. Perfect.

And it wasn't like we were going to hurt the old woman ... we'd just get her out of the joint and burn the damn thing to the ground. Just like the Bidwell Plant. T-Ho hadn't said the part about her being out of the house, but he hadn't said we'd hurt her either. That was good. I didn't want to hurt anybody. I just wanted to pay her back for what she did at the Bidwell Plant ... and for being a Jew.

And maybe forty or fifty years from now, people would walk around where Numbers' house used to be and they'd talk about the day it burned down, just like we'd talked about the day the Bidwell Plant exploded.

Full circle.

Six

No school on the twenty-fourth. Which meant like major sleep-in.

Except I didn't sleep in. Hardly slept at all. Thinking about Mr. R and Numbers and The Six and how I didn't have a girlfriend and had lost my match at the regionals and what Mr. R had said after.

I mean, it wasn't that I wanted to burn somebody's house down. But this wasn't just somebody, this was a *Jew*. What had Mr. R said that day in class? About people being willing to make an unpopular stand because it was the right thing to do? Wasn't that what this was about? If I just had the courage to do it.

Because I was scared — real scared. I was like hands-shaking, swallowing-every-five-seconds, taking-deep-breaths scared.

The day went by slower than any day I could remember. I watched this ancient black-and-white version of *A Christmas Carol* on TV. I tried watching sports after that, but I couldn't get interested. I went for a walk. I *never* go for a walk. And the whole time

I was walking I was looking around like maybe something was going to jump out at me and Give Me The Answer. Like somebody I'd never seen before would walk out of some house and hand me a note that said, "Burn down the house and be somebody." Or there'd be a neon sign in someone's living room window flashing on and off, "Make a stand. Do the right thing."

But there were no signs, no clues. Just a cold wind from the northwest that made me wish I'd worn a heavier coat. A few snowflakes were swirling around in the wind. And there was the smell of Regan's Bakery from around the corner. One of my favourite smells in the world.

What the hell, why not? I went through the front door and saw Mrs. Regan bagging up cinnamon buns and dinner rolls. I looked at the clock. Ten to three. Getting on toward closing time and I figured with the holidays coming people would be able to buy the buns at a discount for the rest of the afternoon.

Mrs. Regan smiled at me. "Hello, Andy. What's the weather doing out there?"

"Looks like it might get a bit wintery," I told her.

"Just in time for Christmas."

She went back to bagging buns. Mrs. Regan never rushed you. I liked that. She just let you look around and decide what you wanted. Mr. Regan was a different story. Big hurry if he was behind the counter. And it didn't matter how many jelly donuts you bought, he gave you one napkin. Like a second napkin would break the outfit.

"I'll have one of those glazed donuts ... and how much are the bags of cinnamon buns?"

"Two dollars. And I'll throw in the donut. It's Christmas."

"Thanks." I pulled a five out of my pocket and handed it to her.

She handed me my change, the cinnamon buns, and my donut in a piece of wax paper. And three napkins.

"Thanks," I said again.

"Merry Christmas." She smiled at me and bobbed her head up and down.

"Merry Christmas, Mrs. Regan. And to Mr. Regan, too."

The door opened and more people came into the bakery so I waited until they passed me before stepping back outside. I stood a few feet from the front of the bakery and downed the donut in three bites. I realized it was the first thing I'd eaten that day.

I walked back home and gave my mom the cinnamon buns. "A little pre-Christmas surprise," I told her. Actually I hadn't spent much more on her actual present, or Dad's or my brother's. But they never seemed to mind.

Dinner was like a slow-motion replay of "Worst Plays of the Week." I knocked over my water, dropped my fork on the floor, and had to be asked three times to pass the peas before I realized Dad was talking to me.

"Christmas excitement," Mom said.

Yeah, that's it.

In a way it *was* excitement. I'd never done anything like what we were going to do that night and I was a little scared and a whole lot nervous. I kept trying to think what the whole thing would be like. T-Ho hadn't said anything about how we'd do it. What would my part be? Would I be the one to lure her out of the house? Or would I start the fire? And if I did — with what? Matches? Did people use matches to start houses on fire? Maybe gasoline?

After supper I helped with the dishes. Mom was chattering away about Christmas and kept saying she hoped I'd been a good boy or Santa wouldn't be coming by. Most years that was pretty funny but this year I was having trouble seeing the humour. A couple of times I tried to smile, but I didn't say anything.

Then it was time to go. I had to figure out what to wear. What does somebody wear when they're going to burn someone's house down? I stared into my closet for a while. I decided on the dark blue hoodie I got for my birthday (I would have preferred black, but I didn't have one), a sort of army-looking green toque, and a dark brown jacket that was too light for how cold it was but I picked it because it was the darkest jacket I had. I figured dark was good.

At the front door I yelled to Mom that I wouldn't be long (how long could it take to start a fire?) and hurried out to the driveway before she could answer. I climbed into the driver's seat of the Biscayne and stared at the dash for quite a while before I put the key in the ignition. The engine was cold and the inside of the car wasn't any warmer. The windows weren't frosted over, though, so I didn't have to wait for the Biscayne's heater to warm up.

I drove slower than I usually do all the way to the dairy. I parked the Biscayne on a side road — the closest one to the dairy — and kept the motor running. The car had a good heater and it was all right inside by then. I rolled the window down — my dad told me to do that whenever you let a vehicle idle, just in case carbon monoxide gets in.

The smell from the dairy was bad that night — real bad. I'd driven this way a lot of times and some days were worse than others, but this was one of the worst. The smell of cow shit and urine came in through my nose and eventually settled in every part of my body.

It was cloudy so there was no moon and no stars. I nodded like that was all part of the plan. What plan? Were we going to sneak up and pour gasoline on one of the walls, light it, and run like hell? Or go in there screaming like banshees to scare the old lady out of her house and then throw in a lit gasoline-soaked towel wrapped around a stick? And then watch the place go up? I realized I had no freaking idea what was going to happen in the next hour of my life. I also realized this was the second time in the last couple of hours that I had asked myself the same questions. Except this time I'd asked them out loud. Talking to myself. And drumming my fingers on the steering wheel.

Christmas excitement. Headlights appeared on the highway coming from my left — the direction of town. Could be them. I watched the lights and listened. I figured I'd recognize the sound of the Crap Wagon. And I did. It was coming fast.

T-Ho and Rebel went past me without slowing down. The only window that worked in the Crap Wagon was open and they were screaming or singing or something. Whatever it was, it was loud. Apparently our plan didn't involve sneaking up on Numbers' house. Turns out they did see me because Rebel gave the finger out his window, then signalled like I should follow.

I put the Biscayne in gear, pulled out onto the highway, and started after them. Except I went like a snail and even kept the volume down on my radio. I knew it was stupid, bothering to be quiet with the decibels of a Radiohead concert and the Indianapolis 500 leading the way.

I didn't speed up either. I wasn't sure why. I still wanted to be part of this — to not miss the opportunity, as Mr. R had put it — but the way T-Ho and Rebel were going about it didn't make sense to me. This wasn't supposed to be a party, was it? Wasn't this all about evening a score for what had happened at the Bidwell Plant? Weren't we making a stand, doing the right thing, striking a blow against the wannabe world dominators — the Jews? I'd thought we were doing something serious — something important.

I kept driving and eventually came to the turn-off into Numbers' place. I turned into the driveway and the sound of my tires crunching over the gravel sounded like a couple dozen uzis all firing at once. There were trees all around the driveway and they opened up into a sort of big yard. I wondered about the stories I'd heard, saying what a crap house the old lady lived in — an "eyesore," everyone said. The thing is, no one would be able to see the house unless they actually drove into the yard.

It was dark so it was hard to tell, but the yard didn't look like one of those well-kept places that in the summer would have the lawn and trees totally looked after. T-Ho and Rebel had parked in about the middle of the yard and they weren't singing or hollering or whatever the hell they'd been doing earlier. I was glad. Maybe they'd come to their senses, were taking the thing seriously. Which is how I was pretty sure Mr. R would have wanted it.

Except I was wrong. I watched them bail out of the Crap Wagon, laughing like they'd just heard Hennie's best joke ever. Then they walked around to the front of the Crap Wagon and stopped, still laughing and staring at the house. Laughing, but not as loud. T-Ho was holding a propane torch. It was attached to a propane bottle and Rebel was carrying that. I got out of the Biscayne and came around in front of them, my back to the house. Rebel glanced at me for maybe a tenth of a second and T-Ho didn't look at me at all.

"Rea-dy?" T-Ho dragged the word out. He was grinning but still not looking at me. I didn't know if he was talking to Rebel or me or both of us.

"How are we going to make sure she's not in there?" I kept my voice at just above a whisper.

Neither one answered. I turned and looked at Numbers' house. It was two storeys, but not real big and definitely not fancy. Even in the dark there was enough light to show the place needed painting. Looked like it had needed painting for a long time. So maybe you could call it an eyesore.

A couple of steps led up to a porch that ran along the front of the house. There were a few lights on inside. But the part that freaked me out was the light on the porch. It was on, too — like the old lady was expecting company or something. Like maybe someone might drop by on Christmas Eve. Then I remembered she was a Jew, and I recalled reading somewhere that Jews don't celebrate Christmas. Still, the light bothered me.

The dairy smell was less here in the yard, but the place was no daisy patch. I looked back at T-Ho and Rebel. "If she's at home, how do we get her out of there?" I still wasn't clear on that part.

They started toward the house and as they passed me, T-Ho looked at me and winked. Another smell. Not as powerful as the cow shit but there. Definitely there. T-Ho and Rebel had been drinking ... this time a fair amount.

"That'd be a real good job for the Alamo man," T-Ho said, a lot louder than I figured was a good idea.

I started after them. "How the hell do I...?" That's as far as I got.

Because that's when the night took a turn I hadn't expected. I guess if you'd asked what was the last thing I figured would happen when we got to Numbers' house, I might have said having the old Jew lady walk onto the porch to face us. That would have been right up there. But it was the other part that freaked me a whole lot more.

The other part was that Patti Bailer was standing beside her.

Seven

T-Ho and Rebel stopped walking. For the first time I noticed how quiet it was. Without the rumble of the Crap Wagon and loud voices laughing and jarring the stillness, it was like the night I'd been at the Bidwell Plant. Totally quiet.

Silent night.

For some reason what people were wearing seemed like a big deal. T-Ho and Rebel had been on the same page as me when it came to house-burning attire. T-Ho: dark blue hoodie (hood up), jeans, some kind of work boots. Rebel: brown leather jacket, toque (the new one), jeans (real dark, almost black), and brown sneakers. He was wearing gloves. On the porch, the old lady was wearing a housecoat — light blue, not fancy — wrapped around some kind of pants that covered her legs. Even from where I was standing she looked like she was shivering. But maybe it was shaking — scared. I couldn't tell.

Patti was wearing a yellow, almost gold, sweatshirt — University of Colorado with a big buffalo head on it. Ball cap, light green, no writing on it. Yoga pants, white runners. She looked like she could be getting ready to go jogging. Except that as I looked at her I could tell there was nothing that would make her run anywhere. She was staying on that porch, no matter what.

I actually felt like I was going to puke. I know people say that but I could taste bile in my mouth and it was like my stomach had clenched itself into a ball. I thought about sneaking back to the Biscayne and trying to slink out of there without being seen, but I abandoned that thought in about three seconds. I knew Patti had seen me. My stomach stayed clenched as everybody stood still, looking at each other and saying exactly nothing.

Patti had her arms crossed and there was a little smile at the corners of her mouth. It wasn't a friendly smile.

"I wondered if you'd really do this," she said. I think she said it to T-Ho but she was looking at me.

T-Ho must have thought Patti was talking to him too because he snorted and laughed a little laugh. "You and the Jew better get your asses off that porch or be ready to get cooked like a couple of marshmallows." He took a few steps forward, not big ones. Rebel was pretty much in step beside him.

I didn't think T-Ho had chosen the best word. There was nothing about Patti that was anything like a marshmallow. And Numbers might have been afraid, but she wasn't exactly diving for cover. Neither of them had moved. And neither looked like she was about to.

"Hello, Andy."

Hearing Patti say my name made me feel even shittier that I already felt.

"Yeah … hi."

"You, too? You going to be part of the big house burning? Must take amazing courage to burn down an old person's home."

T-Ho and Rebel stopped walking toward the house.

"How do you know … about …" My voice didn't sound like me.

Patti laughed. "Your friends were bragging at school yesterday about what they were going to do." She looked at T-Ho, the smile, if that's what it was, still on her face. "And look at you — you're really going to do it. Liquid courage. And maybe something more, a little weed … mushrooms or crack maybe? Yeah, you gotta love bravery, right men?"

The way she said "men" didn't make me feel all that manly. I wanted to tell Patti that I hadn't been drinking, but I didn't think she'd care. I couldn't tell what T-Ho and Rebel were thinking but they didn't move.

I took one step closer to the porch. "What are you doing here?"

Patti looked at me, not laughing or smiling now. "What's wrong? Does it cramp your style that the old lady isn't all alone? It happens I volunteer. I visit seniors, read to them, talk to them, *listen* to them — you should try it, Andy. It's amazing what you can learn."

After a while T-Ho pointed. "That bitch set fire to the Bidwell Plant." He spat the words at Patti. "People died in that fire, or don't you give a shit about that? Then the Jew made it look like she saved a guy that was hurt — but the only reason he was hurt was because she started the fire in the first place."

Patti stepped down onto the top stair of the porch. She turned and looked back at Numbers and held out her hand. I could hear her say, "It's okay" in a really soft voice and after a few seconds, the old lady moved down to where she was.

Patti turned back to us. "You might want to check your facts. There was an investigation of the Bidwell fire right after it happened. A gas leak caused the explosion. Julia got out safely but she went back in to help the man who was injured — she saved his life."

"Bullshit." T-Ho barked at the porch.

"Good answer." Patti nodded and laughed again. "Oh, and one other thing that you might not know. The man she saved? His last name was Retzlaff. As in your Mr. R's grandfather."

When Patti said that, I was pretty sure I saw the old lady — Numbers — nod. It was just the smallest nod but it was there.

"I don't get it."

"You know what, Andy?" Patti was looking at me again. It seemed she was looking at me a lot of the time. "I believe you. I believe that you don't get it. But they do." Her eyes finally left me and she stared hard at T-Ho and Rebel.

"Don't you, boys? All those intimate conversations with Mr. R — oh, I know about that too — saw the three of you together a couple of times. Except I'll just bet Mr. R, the Jew-hater, never mentioned that his grandfather was the person Julia dragged out of the Bidwell Plant. How much do you think he hated having a Jew save his grandpa? He might never have said *that* to you, but I'll bet it ate him up."

It felt like the night was the quietest it had been since we got there. No sound but people breathing.

"You people are pathetic. All three of you." She looked at me again when she said that last part.

When Patti stopped speaking, Numbers — the woman called Julia — inched a little closer to her. I could see that she was squeezing Patti's hand. But Patti's eyes never left T-Ho or Rebel ... or me.

I glanced over at T-Ho and Rebel. It didn't look like either of them knew what to do.

It was like they'd read my mind and decided to act. They both started moving forward, T-Ho talking as he moved. "Enough of this crap. We're burning this piece of shit down. So move. Now!"

Patti didn't move. Numbers looked at Patti then back at us. She didn't move either. She wasn't shaking anymore.

"That makes no sense," I said.

"What doesn't?" Patti looked at me.

"Why would Mr. R want to hurt someone who saved his grandpa's life? Even if she was a Jew."

T-Ho and Rebel hesitated, maybe waiting to hear what Patti would say.

"You're right," she nodded "It makes exactly zero sense … unless you hate Jewish people so much that you're ashamed that someone in your family was actually saved by a Jew. Unless you hate Jews so much that you would rather your grandfather had died than be saved by one."

I thought back to that day at the regionals, the day I'd lost to the kid named Epstein. Mr. R had been pretty pissed off … not that I'd lost, but about the person I'd lost to. *You don't ever let those people beat you.*

"Oh, and one more thing." Patti reached down and took Numbers by the hand. She held up the old woman's arm and pushed the sleeve of her housecoat back to her elbow. There was something on Numbers' left forearm … like a tattoo. I wasn't close enough to read it.

It didn't matter. Patti read it for us. "8-5-2-3-9." She said each number slowly and looked up at us after each one. "Did you ever wonder why Julia is called 'Numbers'? Let me help you with that. This is the number she was given when she was sent to the Auschwitz concentration camp in Poland. In a way, having this number tattooed on her arm was a good thing, because when people arrived at Auschwitz, there was a selection process. Children, their mothers, the old, the sick, and the weak — they didn't get numbers. I guess the Nazis figured it would be a waste of time since they were immediately marched away to die. Julia was strong, so she was sent off to the work camp. She lived. Most didn't."

"What a bunch of shit," Rebel said, but he didn't say it very loud.

"You're right," Patti nodded. "It is shit to Holocaust deniers," Patti stared hard at Rebel. "It's all crap to Retzlaff … and to you three." Her voice dropped down when she said "and to you three." "To the rest of us, it's the most horrible mass murder ever."

It was weird but I wasn't thinking about mass murder or whether there really had been a Holocaust or not. I was thinking about *and to you three*. I'd never made it into The Six but here I was part of a different number. A smaller number. But I was part of it.

I took a couple of steps closer to the porch. I don't know why but it was suddenly important for me to see the old woman's arm — to read the numbers for myself. She still had her arm extended. I could see them now: 8-5-2-3-9. I looked up at the woman and realized for the first time how old she actually was. Or at least how old she looked. Which was really old. She was Patti's height or close to it, and very thin. Didn't look strong at all. But sixty years ago she must have been stronger. Strong enough to get Mr. R's grandfather out of a burning plant. To save his life.

Sixty years. It was that long ago that the Bidwell Plant had blown up. That had to make her somewhere in her eighties. I stared at the old woman Patti had called Julia. She didn't look evil; she just looked old. And tired.

"Crap." T-Ho said it this time but it was like nobody was listening.

I took another step closer to the porch.

"How about it, Andy?"

I was concentrating so hard on the numbers on that skin-and-bones arm I almost didn't hear Patti. What had she said ... "how about it, Andy?"

How about it, Andy what? But I knew what she meant. Was I going to stay with Rebel and T-Ho or was I going to walk away? What was I going to do?

I mean, it didn't take a damn rocket scientist to figure out we couldn't burn the house down now. There were witnesses, for Christ's sake. The old woman lowered her arm but Patti was still holding her hand. They looked out at us. Nobody moved. Nobody spoke.

And that's when I knew. This wasn't about starting or not starting a fire. It was about exactly what Mr. R had taught us. It was about not just accepting what was said. It was about deciding for yourself.

Somehow, it was like T-Ho knew what was going on in my head. "A-la-mo, don't you go forgettin' that this is your chance ... your big chance to be *jen-yoo-wine*, Alamo boy."

I looked back at him and Rebel, still holding the torch and the propane bottle. To tell the truth, they *did* look kind of pathetic: Ready to burn down a house that probably wasn't worth much more than the Crap Wagon and that belonged to an old woman who looked like she'd have trouble swatting flies.

I stepped up onto the top stair of the porch and turned to face T-Ho and Rebel. I was a little ways away from Patti. I remember having this weird thought — if this was a movie Patti would hold out her other hand

and I'd take it and it would make this amazing final scene.

But life isn't a movie … it's just life. Patti didn't hold out her hand or even look at me. T-Ho and Rebel started toward the house but I knew they weren't thinking about setting fire to the place anymore. It was about me now. I figured I was about to find out how tough I was when I wasn't on a wrestling mat.

Patti reached into her pocket and pulled out her cellphone. "You two are even stupider than I thought. And to be honest, I've always thought you were pretty stupid. Did you really think we'd be standing out here waiting for you without calling the cops first? They'll be here any second and we're sure going to miss you when you go."

At first I wasn't sure T-Ho and Rebel were going to stop. And I didn't know if Patti really had called the cops. I listened for a siren off in the distance but I didn't hear anything.

I don't know if T-Ho believed Patti or not but he stopped. He stared at me for what seemed like a really long time. Then he laughed.

"I was right all along, you puke piece of shit. You ain't never going to be *jen-yoo-wine*."

I was still trying to think of what to say to that when I did hear the siren. It was still a long way off but T-Ho and Rebel heard it too. And they turned away, walked to the Crap Wagon, threw the torch and propane bottle in the back seat, jumped in the car, and roared away.

190

That's when the old Jew lady named Julia spoke for the first time. Not to me. Not even to Patti. It was like she was directing her words to the car that was spinning gravel and speeding out of her yard.

"Why do you hate me?" she said in a small voice that I could only hear because I was on the porch with her. "Why do you hate all of us?"

I stood on the porch and watched the Crap Wagon disappear through the trees and out onto the highway.

Patti said, "Thanks, Andy," and she and Numbers — Julia — turned and walked back into the house.

SEPTEMBER

ONE YEAR LATER

Epilogue

It didn't go away quietly. Or quickly.

T-Ho and Rebel got probation and community service. And they were suspended from school for the rest of that year. They're back now, but they don't bother me. Not anymore. At first I thought I'd get the crap beaten out of me by someone in The Six but that didn't happen. Maybe they figured that what would happen to them if they did that wasn't worth it.

Besides, they had a better idea. Another fire. But this time they actually got it done. There was even a pretty major explosion that went along with it — like the Bidwell Plant.

Full circle.

I'd filled up the Biscayne with gas the night before so their timing was perfect. By the time the fire department got the fire out, all that was left of my car was a burned out shell. It looked like one of those newscast stories from some car bomb attack somewhere in the Middle East. And whoever started the fire was smart enough to make sure there was no way it could ever be proved. But the four members of The Six that were still at Parkerville made sure they saw me in the halls the day after. Lots of smiles, actually grins ... even a couple of thumbs up.

Patti phoned me when she heard about my car to say how sorry she was but we didn't talk long. I wasn't feeling much like talking to anybody just then.

Insurance paid for it and my dad said we could get another Biscayne. My brother even found one online. But I didn't buy it, didn't want to. I only wanted one Biscayne and it was gone. Now I drive a '97 GM pickup. It's okay.

Garth Redlake came around again too. This time the reporter came to our house. My dad insisted on sitting in. To make sure I didn't say the wrong thing, I guess. But he didn't have to worry — I didn't intend to say much of anything.

The first newspaper story came out about a week after the night at Numbers' house. And even though I wasn't quoted — some kids were — the story definitely made Mr. R look bad. And even after all the stuff that had happened, I didn't like that. I guess I still wanted to believe that the whole thing wasn't his fault. It felt better to think that T-Ho and Rebel had sort of gone off on their own and dreamed up a plan to get revenge on the old lady.

My mom and dad totally disagreed with me on that and so did my brother — he was one of the people who *was* quoted in that article. There were lots more stories after that first one as suddenly Parkerville Comprehensive was like this huge media deal. The school board meetings got more coverage than the United Nations. Even though the meetings that dealt with Mr. R were closed to the public and the media, there were television cameras from the big networks; national newspapers had some of their big name reporters and columnists there, and there were people from different groups too, like the National Jewish Alliance and the Freedom of Speech Forever group and some others that I didn't pay a lot of attention to.

Patti was interviewed tons of times and after a while I'd see her on TV and she looked like she just wanted it all to go away. Maybe that's why her family moved to Toronto right after the year was over.

Mr. R was fired. They called it an "indefinite suspension," but after all the stuff that's been said and written about the guy, I don't think he'll ever teach again. Not around here, that's for sure. I heard he's opened up a computer store but I haven't gone around to see how he's doing.

It's funny in a way, but nobody calls me Alamo this year. It's one of the things that's not part of my life anymore, like Mr. R and Patti and the Biscayne. The difference is, I don't miss "Alamo."

The petition was another part of the whole thing that I guess I won't ever forget. After Mr. R was kicked out of school, some kids organized this petition to get him reinstated. At first I figured it must have been The Six that started it — sort of a way to help Mr. R and show the world that T-Ho and Rebel weren't such bad guys after all. But it wasn't them; it was some grade twelves who were about to graduate. They circulated around the school near the end of June with the petition for kids to sign.

More than half the kids at Parkerville signed it. A grad named Darrell Whitchell approached me one day in the common area when I was eating my lunch. By myself. Which is how I ate lunch most of the time. That day I was working on a banana and trying to get through chapter eighteen of *Moby Dick*. Our last English exam of the year was on that book and to tell the truth I was kind of enjoying it. Maybe it helped me escape from everything that was happening around me. Anyway, that's what I was doing when Darrell sat down and said, "So how about it, Crockett, are you going to sign?"

He stuck the petition down on the table in front of me. I looked at it and right away I could see names of kids that I knew.

I'd been thinking about that petition ever since I'd heard there was one and I wanted to sign it. I'd say I was even looking forward to it. Even though I knew some of the stuff Mr. R had done was wrong, he was still the best teacher I'd ever had. I'd had okay teachers before, but never anybody who had made me look forward to school like Mr. R. He'd made me think about things I'd never thought about in my life. I'd learned stuff that I didn't think could ever matter to me. But it did ... because of Mr. R.

And now he was out of school, probably forever.

"You have to print your name and then sign right next to it. If you put anything else down or don't sign in the right place or anything, you won't count. It won't be genuine."

When he said "genuine" it was like this rushing noise started in my head. I looked up and T-Ho was leaning against a wall, not far away, grinning at me like he had every time he said "*jen-yoo-wine*." He'd been banned from the school but it wasn't like he couldn't get in there if he really wanted to. I guess he figured this was too good to miss.

The rushing noise was getting louder inside my head. And I was seeing all these images: The look on Mr. R's face when he'd said, "The fall of the Alamo" ... Rebel being all curious that day at the ruins of the Bidwell Plant ... Uncle Herm, his face red from drinking or being pissed off or maybe both, practically yelling at me, "There's a few of those guys around — Holocaust deniers is what they're called — and they're all full of shit" ... Mr. R covered with blood lying on the street by that bus ... Patti looking so intense in social studies ... my burned out Biscayne ... an old lady standing on a falling-down porch late at night with the sleeve of her housecoat pulled up and asking in the softest voice, "Why do you hate me?"

I've thought about it a thousand times since and I can't explain why. Why it was that with all those images flashing around like a video on fast forward and the rushing noise getting louder in my head and T-Ho grinning at me and Darrell Whitchell pointing at where I should sign, that I picked up the pen and wrote in the space right next to Darrell Whitchell's finger —

8-5-2-3-9

Available at your favourite bookseller

VISIT US AT

Dundurn.com
@dundurnpress
Facebook.com/dundurnpress
Pinterest.com/dundurnpress